D1649794

Powys
Withdrawn
37218 00360660 0

SPECIAL MESSAGE TO READERS

This book is published under the auspices of

THE ULVERSCROFT FOUNDATION

(registered charity No. 264873 UK)

Established in 1972 to provide funds for research, diagnosis and treatment of eye diseases. Examples of contributions made are: —

A Children's Assessment Unit at Moorfield's Hospital, London.

•

Twin operating theatres at the Western Ophthalmic Hospital, London.

•

A Chair of Ophthalmology at the Royal Australian College of Ophthalmologists.

•

The Ulverscroft Children's Eye Unit at the Great Ormond Street Hospital For Sick Children, London.

You can help further the work of the Foundation by making a donation or leaving a legacy. Every contribution, no matter how small, is received with gratitude. Please write for details to:

THE ULVERSCROFT FOUNDATION,
The Green, Bradgate Road, Anstey,
Leicester LE7 7FU, England.
Telephone: (0116) 236 4325

In Australia write to:
THE ULVERSCROFT FOUNDATION,
c/o The Royal Australian and New Zealand
College of Ophthalmologists,
94-98 Chalmers Street, Surry Hills,
N.S.W. 2010, Australia

TAKE THE OREGON TRAIL

Thousands of men had taken the trail to the west looking for a new beginning — many didn't make it. Adam Trant had also set out on the Oregon Trail — but he was looking for an old enemy. The hunt took him to a savage wilderness and matched him against deadly marauders. Adam was ready to die, as long as he succeeded in his quest. However, he wasn't ready for the unpredictable force of the love of a woman.

Books by Eugene Clifton
in the Linford Western Library:

HANG THE SHERIFF HIGH
RIDE BACK TO REDEMPTION
HIDEOUT
A PLACE CALLED JEOPARDY

EUGENE CLIFTON

TAKE THE OREGON TRAIL

Complete and Unabridged

LINFORD
Leicester

First published in Great Britain in 2010 by
Robert Hale Limited
London

First Linford Edition
published 2012
by arrangement with
Robert Hale Limited
London

British Library CIP Data

Clifton, Eugene.
Take the Oregon trail. - -
(Linford western library)
1. Bounty hunters- -Fiction.
2. Western stories.
3. Large type books.
I. Title II. Series
823.9′2–dc23

ISBN 978–1–4448–1021–9

Published by
F. A. Thorpe (Publishing)
Anstey, Leicestershire

Set by Words & Graphics Ltd.
Anstey, Leicestershire
Printed and bound in Great Britain by
T. J. International Ltd., Padstow, Cornwall

This book is printed on acid-free paper

1

Winter looked to be coming early. Snow clouds hung low over the mountains, their colour a match for the iron grey horse pausing briefly on a ridge. The man who sat in the saddle gazed through narrowed eyes at the terrain, before pushing his mount back into motion. Adam Trant heaved at the lead rope tied to his saddlebow, knowing without looking around that the pack mule was balking again. Cross-grained like many of its kind, when it wasn't trying to break loose the mule was sidling across to kick out at the fine-boned bay he'd brought along as a spare mount.

Once Trant left the trading post at Fort Boise there'd been fewer people on the trail. Most of the westbound emigrants would have reached their destinations by now. Over a week ago he'd shared a pot of coffee with some Oregonians heading east. They'd told him about a slow moving wagon train ahead of him, a group of several hundred souls, mostly Missourians, who had left St Joseph at the beginning of May. 'They're takin' their time,' his informant said. 'They'd been camped in that one spot for near enough two weeks. They'll be lucky to find any boats to take them down the Columbia River.'

'You didn't meet anyone else, maybe some folk who jumped off from Kanesville?' Trant asked. 'I'm looking for two men who left in July, but they'd be travelling light; I doubt if they'd want to throw in with a group moving that slow.'

'We heard tell about a small party, maybe seven or eight wagons, followin' the Fullerton cut-off. I never knew anybody that had any luck on that trail, but there's always folks eager to try anything that might get them to Oregon quicker.'

'One of the men I'm looking for mentioned the Fullerton cut-off,' Trant mused. 'Could be he'd go that way.'

'We've not met two men travelling alone. It's a whole lot safer having company. The Indians around these parts are pretty slick when it comes to stealing horses.'

As he recalled that conversation Trant scanned the landscape. He'd encountered very few natives on his journey, and none of them had been hostile. He'd traded for some meat with a couple of Pawnees only a week out of Kanesville. Later, trying to swim his animals across the River Platte when it was swollen after a storm, he probably would have gotten himself drowned if a group of Sioux hadn't come to his rescue. It had made him disinclined to worry about any further meeting with Indians, but maybe he'd been lucky; the tribes to the west of Salt Lake might not be as peaceable as those in Nebraska.

Once he'd taken to the Fullerton

cut-off Trant hadn't encountered a single soul; he'd travelled plenty over the last few years and he was used to being alone, but there was something about this vast hostile landscape that made him feel uneasy. He was grateful for the signs left by the wagon train, although he guessed it was a couple of weeks ahead of him. There was no way of knowing if Davie Gaunt had brought Sim Morrow this way; Trant was acting on a hunch and, as the days passed by, he began to think of turning around, but he'd be no better off on the main Oregon Trail. Finding two men among the thousands who were heading west had always been a forlorn hope.

Trant's thoughts began to drift until he was no longer seeing the ground beneath the grey's hoofs; his mind was journeying elsewhere, taking him back to Iowa. As his eyes drifted shut a woman's voice echoed in Trant's head, as it had so often these past weeks, sleeping and waking.

'What have you done? How could

you?' She had been too anguished for tears, pushed far beyond weeping. 'Leave me alone, Adam. I never want to see you again. Never.' As he slumped in the saddle, Trant's mouth twisted, the lines round eyes and mouth deepening. For a moment he didn't notice that the mule and the bay were dragging back; the grey slowed, its nostrils flaring.

They were approaching a boulder field, with rocks large enough to hide a mounted man, and the horse snorted uneasily. Trant returned to the present as something rattled away from the horse's feet, making a hollow sound. It was a human skull.

It wasn't uncommon to find human remains along the trail, yet the sight made Adam Trant bring the grey to a halt. His mount was restless; when an unpleasant sickly scent reached Trant's less sensitive nostrils he knew why. It wasn't the presence of this bare bone that was troubling the horse, but the smell of decaying flesh.

Trant lit down from the saddle and

tethered the animals to a spike of rock. He started forward on foot, treading softly, his ears and eyes stretched, his nose wrinkling as the stench grew stronger. He turned around a rocky spur and came across the ruins of a wagon lying across the trail, burnt out to a heap of charred wood and twisted metal. A dozen paces further on Trant found himself in the middle of a graveyard. More bones lay scattered amongst the row of piled rocks, not all of them totally stripped of flesh; scavengers had been at work where the bodies hadn't been well enough covered. Sombrely, Trant counted the rough heaps of stone; eight people had been buried here. One skull, with skin and hair still clinging to it, was split almost in two, while a long bone lying nearby had been shattered by a powerful blow; these people had died violent deaths.

Clamping down on the nausea rising in his throat at the task, Trant dug among the graves. Once he was satisfied that the two men he had travelled so far to find weren't among the dead, he piled rocks over the bodies again; it seemed the right thing to do, though the scavengers would soon return.

Lost in dark thoughts, Trant headed back to the horses, halting abruptly as they came into view. A man was standing by the mule, one hand on the animal's neck, the other reaching to the pack on its back. What might once have been a flannel shirt hung in tatters from the man's shoulders, his beard and hair were long and tangled, and his head was bare. His feet were bare too, bluish white with cold and speckled with dried blood.

'Looks like you've been through some bad times,' Trant said quietly, as the stranger spun around. 'Take it easy, mister. There's food and fresh coffee in that pack, why don't I get us a fire going.' Bright blue eyes burnt in a face deeply slashed by an angry scar and dried blood matted the greying beard. The mouth, with lips scabbed and oozing, had a strand of spittle hanging from it.

'Take it easy,' Trant repeated, reaching out a placating hand, seeing nothing but an unreasoning hatred in the stranger's constantly moving eyes.

'Where are they? Tell me!' The words tumbling from him, the man clawed beneath the tatters of his clothes, as if he was searching for something. His voice rose to a bubbling scream. 'What have you done with them?' He launched himself at Trant, his hand coming up to strike. Clutched in his fingers was a long rusty blade.

Trant made a grab at his six-gun, but his fingers encountered only the skirt of the long coat he wore against the cold, and came up empty. There was barely time to bring his arm across, to block the killing blow. Trant had lived long enough to learn how to use his fists, but he'd never fought a man so clearly intent on murder. The rusty blade slammed into his forearm, and Trant staggered under the blow. He stumbled, and before he had time to recover, the madman came leaping after him, the blade drawn back for another attack, this one intended to drive between his ribs.

Twisting in desperation, Trant managed to close his hands around the fist that held the knife. His balance had gone, and they both fell, rolling together, but he clung on; he could feel the warmth of his blood dripping fast from the wound in his arm. He couldn't afford to let in another thrust or the fight could only have one end.

Ignoring the madman's free hand which was battering at his skull, Trant smashed the captive arm against a rock, intent on breaking the man's grip and removing the knife from his grasp. His opponent began to make a high-pitched keening sound, eyes wide and staring, his lips drawn back over broken teeth, the weird noise issuing from between them sounding more animal than human.

Trant took a chance, relinquishing

his grip with his right hand to drive it into his opponent's belly. The air rushed from the man's lungs in an audible whoosh, and the extraordinary strength he had shown seemed to go out of him; he made no attempt to resist as Trant eased the blade from his hand.

'Are there more of you?' Trant asked, grabbing the ragged remains of the shirt and pulling the man's head up. 'Were you the one who buried those people? What happened to the rest of the wagons?'

He got no reply. The man went limp in Trant's grasp, covering his face with his hands. His anger draining away, Trant let him go. The rusty blade was stained with his blood; he picked up a rock and broke it into three pieces, tossing them away. He climbed into the saddle, wincing as the wound in his arm began to throb.

When Trant rode away the madman still sat slumped in a heap, rocking himself and sobbing quietly into his hands as if he'd forgotten his adversary's existence.

Pretty soon Trant found another wagon, lying drunkenly on its side, with the remains of an animal still harnessed to it; so much of the rotting body was missing that Trant couldn't tell whether it had been a horse or a mule.

Somebody had been scavenging, taking firewood, and probably carving meat from the carcass, and there were fresh boot prints over the whole area, made by several different sized feet. Trant followed the tracks until they disappeared on a great humped shelf of bare rock.

'Hello,' Trant called. 'Is anybody there?'

There was silence, broken only by the faint rustle of the wind. Then, as suddenly as if she had sprung from thin air, a woman appeared on the crest of the hill.

'John? Is that you?' She came running, hitching her skirts high, a gaunt figure with greying hair escaping from under a dusty black bonnet. 'Where are — ' she broke off, seeing him clearly as she drew closer.

'Guess I'm not who you were expecting, ma'am, but it looks like you folks are in trouble. If there's anything I can do I'm willing to help.'

'You're alone?' She stared over his head, before her gaze returned to Trant. 'Did you meet John? Or Mr Blazy?'

'I've seen no one in a good long time. Last people I met came from Oregon, and they told me some wagons had taken this trail.' Behind her three more women were hurrying down the slope, accompanied by a scatter of children. Then came a man, leaning heavily on a stick and making hard work of it. He was fair and slightly built, and Trant studied him with sudden interest, but the man was a stranger, his hair not yellow, but grey with age.

Trant turned back to the woman. 'I was looking for somebody who might have come this way. When I found the graves and the wagons down the trail I realized you'd had some trouble.'

'We're stranded here. Four of our menfolk went to fetch help. My husband and young Tom Pross aimed to go back to Fort Boise, and Mr Blazy and his son headed west. You're sure you didn't meet them?'

'No, ma'am, but it's possible we missed each other somehow,' Trant replied. 'What happened here?'

'We were attacked, more than two weeks ago now. They stole all our livestock.'

'Indians?'

'Not unless Indians have started sprouting beards.' It was the man who answered. He looked as if he'd shed a lot of flesh in a short time, and his face was pale under weathering that spoke of a life spent out of doors. His thigh was wrapped in a bandage that was black with dried blood. 'There was a few braves among 'em, and they'd dressed themselves up with feathers and paint, but mostly they was white.'

'From what I saw back there it

looked as if you had a war on your hands.' Trant said.

'They'd have killed us all if we hadn't found the cave,' one of the women put in. 'We've been afraid they might come back.'

'We've nothing left worth stealing,' the man said, 'except our lives, and we ain't letting them go cheap.'

'If that's so then you can't afford to stay here much longer,' Trant said, nodding at the clouds hanging threateningly low over the mountains. 'Snow could be coming early this year, and it's quite a way back to the Oregon Trail.'

'I've been telling them that this past week,' the man growled, glancing at the women gathered around him. 'Trouble is we don't have so much as a lame mule left, and they wouldn't leave anybody behind.'

'But we're safe here,' the woman said decidedly. 'My husband, Mr John Littleton, promised to bring help from Fort Boise.'

'Unless he's right on my tail he could

be too late.' Trant lifted his head; the air was growing colder and the wind carried the scent of snow. 'How many casualties have you got up there?'

'Only one now, two of those who were hurt in the raid have died. It was touch and go with Mr Tucker here, until a few days ago,' the woman replied. 'Mrs Jewett isn't exactly a casualty, but we can't move her now. She can't walk, and I doubt if she could sit on a horse.'

'Both the wagons I saw were wrecked. Aren't there any others, maybe one we can fix?' Trant asked.

Tucker's eyes lit up. 'Mister, we got just the thing. Blazy's rig ain't much of a wagon, but it's real light.'

With a quick nod, Trant slid himself across from the grey onto the bay's bare back.

'You fit to ride out there and show me?' he invited, reaching to untie the lead rope and gesturing at the empty saddle.

Tucker needed no persuading. 'Sure

glad you happened along, I didn't see no way we were going to get out of here,' he said, offering his hand. 'My friends call me Tuck.'

'Adam. Adam Trant. Is that leg of yours healing, Tuck?' he asked, seeing that the motion of the horse was causing the man some pain.

'It's a whole lot better than it was. I ain't complaining, I was one of the lucky ones.' His face was suddenly grim. 'They killed a kid, Adam, and three women. Wasn't no need for that. Pair of girls went missing too, sisters, real purty. Reckon they must've taken 'em along. Sure would like to catch up with them varmints.'

'We'll have our hands full getting the rest of the women and children out of here alive,' Trant replied. 'There are soldiers patrolling the Oregon Trail — maybe they'll deal with the raiders. What exactly is wrong with this Mrs Jewett? Why isn't she fit to travel?'

'Baby's due any time now, she's been real poorly since her husband died in the raid. Her pains started yesterday.' Tucker gave Trant a rueful glance. 'Could be even if we get this wagon fixed up and ready to roll, them women ain't gonna let us put her in it.'

'Then the whole lot of us are likely to starve up here, unless you've got a stash of food you've been keeping quiet about.'

'Nope. Enough for a week, maybe,' Tuck replied, 'so long as we keep our belts drawn tight.'

'Then we'd better hope that baby puts in an appearance soon.'

2

With less than an hour of daylight left, Trant drew the wagon to a halt, as close as he could get to the hump of rock where the survivors had made their refuge. The horses had never worked in harness before, and he had his hands full; for the first time since he set out he was glad of the mule, standing quiet beside the bay.

He left Tuck to take care of the animals and took the rocky slope at a run, calling to the women as he approached. 'Wagon's ready. We're taking food, blankets and warm clothing, nothing else.'

'Mrs Jewett can't be moved.' Mrs Littleton stood at the cave entrance, her mouth a tight line in the gaunt face, her arms folded across her chest. 'If the baby comes in the next couple of hours then maybe she can travel in the morning.'

'It could snow tonight,' Trant said. He pushed his way around her, blinking in the sudden darkness.

'She's here.' This was a new voice, deep for a woman, yet with a musical quality that twisted something beneath Trant's ribs.

A moan came from the bundle of blankets almost at his feet. Trant hunkered down beside the woman, his eyes making out the white blur of her face. 'Mrs Jewett? We need to get going. I can carry you to the wagon.'

There was a mutter of disapproval from behind him, but Trant ignored it. 'If we stay here another day, you and the baby may die.'

'I'll come,' she whispered. 'I can walk, if you'll help — ' She was suddenly silenced and breathed in sharply, her face twisting in pain. Trant bit his lip, not knowing what to do, but after a few moments she relaxed with a weary sigh. She reached for his hand. 'Help me up; it'll be a while before the next one.'

'Better let the gentleman carry you, him being so much stronger than all us poor feeble womenfolk.' The voice from the shadows was mocking. Trant stared into the dark. 'I mean it, Emma,' the unseen woman said, her voice gentle now. 'You should save your strength.'

'If you'll take my other hand, maybe I can manage.' Mrs Jewett pushed back the blankets, and then the hidden woman moved into the light. Despite himself, Trant drew in a sharp breath.

She was tall, a vision in a peacock blue satin dress that accentuated her generous curves. Borders of lace, once white but now badly stained, hung at her wrists and around her neck. Her clothes were outrageously out of place in the wilderness, but once he'd got over the shock Trant barely noticed; despite the captivating shape of this woman, it was her face that held his gaze. Large dark eyes stared challengingly at him from beneath arched brows; her full lips were curved in a slight smile. She was impossibly beautiful.

'I thought you said we were in a hurry,' she said. She was laughing at him, and he guessed she was used to the effect she had on men. Without a word, Trant scooped Mrs Jewett into his arms and carried her out of the cave. The other women moved aside, their expressions disapproving.

'Anyone who isn't ready in five minutes can stay behind,' Trant said harshly. 'If you're coming, pack up the food and blankets.'

Trant deposited Mrs Jewett in the wagon, followed by the woman in the silk dress; in the fading daylight she looked even more exotic, a blue jay amongst a flock of crows. Dark hair flowed to her shoulders; even in the dull light he could see rich veins of red shining in its depths. Everything about this woman intrigued and aroused him; he wanted to sink his hands into that gleaming mane, pull her to him and explore the inviting fullness of her lips.

Forcing his mind back to the matter in hand, Trant checked the ties securing the sparse canvas cover to the frame; he and Tucker had done their best, but it had been hard to find anything large enough left after the attack. He got the women and children moving. The woman in blue, who had climbed down from the wagon, was trying to contain her hair in a wispy yellow scarf.

'Best get started, ma'am,' he said. 'Tuck will give you a call if you're needed.'

She gave an irritated toss of her fine head, as if she considered she had no need of instruction. Mrs Littleton brought supplies, including a haunch of fresh meat. 'That doesn't look as if it came from the rotting carcass I saw down the trail,' Trant commented. 'Have some of you taken to hunting?'

'It was a gift,' Mrs Littleton replied, turning away to hurry back to the cave. 'I've just one more load to fetch. I shan't be a moment.'

'A gift?' Trant queried, looking at Tucker.

'Bart Wilkie left it. Guess I wasn't thinking about Wilkie when I told you I was the only man left. It was his daughters got snatched by the raiders. That an' a crack on the skull that knocked him cold for a couple of days drove him clear out of his head, but now and then he gets his senses back. When he ain't feeling bad he goes after meat and leaves it outside the cave. He's pretty good with a rifle; that's the third lot he's brought in. Mrs Littleton went looking for him this morning, with some hot stew and coffee, but she never got near enough to give it to him. Seems he ran off at the sight of her. She said he'd gone kinda loco again, and it looked like he'd lost his gun.'

'Reckon that's no bad thing,' Trant said, relating the story of his own encounter with the madman. 'If he'd had a better weapon than a blunt knife I doubt I'd have lived long enough to find you people. He was keen to see me dead, and he wasn't about to listen to reason.'

Tuck shook his head. 'I hear he's crazy one minute, close on normal the next. He's safe enough with the women folk, but when he sees a man he figures it's one of them devils who stole his girls.'

'What happened is enough to drive any man over the edge,' Trant conceded, 'but I'm not eager to meet him again. Dressed the way he is, you'd think he'd have died of cold.'

'I'd say that would suit him just fine, won't have to think no more about what those varmints might be doing to his daughters,' Tuck replied bleakly. He roused himself, sitting straighter as Mrs Littleton came back down the slope. 'Looks like we're ready to go.'

'Take care of this crack team of mine,' Trant said, grinning. He hurried to meet the woman and was surprised to see that she had returned dragging a contraption of poles, rope and canvas.

'Mr Tucker just about got this

finished,' she said.

'A travois.' Trant took it from her.

'Is that what it's called? I think he had an idea we could use it to move Mrs Jewett if we had to leave. You said we mustn't take any extra weight, but if something happened to the wagon it could be useful.'

'It might at that,' Trant nodded. 'I'll tie it on the back. Is that everything?'

'Yes. I left a message in the cave, in case anybody comes looking for us.'

'We'll keep our eyes peeled for a relief mission,' Trant assured her, roping the travois into place. 'It'll be over a week before we get clear of this cut-off and back to the main trail.'

'I'm sure John will be on his way by now,' Mrs Littleton said, looking up at him, her faded eyes challenging. 'We can all go back to Fort Boise and winter there; it's pointless trying to get to Oregon so late in the year.'

'There'll be time enough to think about that when we reach the trail. Even this late, with luck there'll be other folks travelling. Get that team moving, Tuck.' Trant looked in at the woman lying in the wagon bed. 'We're on our way, Mrs Jewett, are you ready?'

For an answer she nodded, her face white.

'Fine. I'll be staying close to the wagon, rounding up the strays. If you need your friend you only have to call and I'll go fetch her.'

* * *

Trant prowled uneasily between the fire and the tethered horses, watching for the first signs of light in the western sky. As he passed the wagon the shadows cast by the lantern shifted, and one of the women within made the canvas bulge as she pushed by. He heard Mrs Jewett's low moan. Two more female figures, unrecognizable in the darkness, were draped over the tailgate; presumably there wasn't room for them to fit inside. It seemed only the children still slept, tucked up in a row beneath

Tucker's travois, which had been upturned against a rock and covered with a blanket to give them a shelter; they'd have had no rest beneath the wagon.

Tucker lay almost under the hoofs of the mule, swathed in his bedroll. 'Ain't easy to listen to,' he remarked, as Trant approached him yet again.

'No,' Trant said shortly. All night he'd been tormented by thoughts of another woman, back in Iowa, and the child she'd borne just days before he left. The boy had hair so fair that it shone like silver. He turned abruptly on his heel, deepening the well worn path back to the fire, and helped himself to coffee, ignoring Mrs Littleton as she lifted a steaming kettle from the flames.

A faint wail filled the pre-dawn silence. Trant's head jerked up and he held his breath, waiting. Another cry came, stronger this time, then a babble of sound from the wagon. 'It's a girl,' came the call, followed by a chorus of subdued congratulations.

Trant threw his coffee grounds into the fire. Looking to the west, he saw a line of brightness; there was snow on top of the mountains. The morning had brought another life that had become his responsibility, one that might last no more than a few days unless their luck held.

Within an hour they were on the move, the wagon lurching slowly downhill. The brief spell of clear weather had passed, and heavy clouds pursued them. Trant resumed his place alongside the rear of the wagon, chivvying those who lagged behind. The woman in the blue silk dress stayed close by, her finery now covered by an Indian blanket and her bright hair hidden under a wrapping of thick black cloth, salvaged when they passed the wrecked wagon the day before; he couldn't help wondering if she had realized the effect she had on him.

A boy, half-grown, came to walk at Trant's side, taking exaggerated steps in an attempt to match his long-legged stride. 'Have your horses got names, mister?'

'The grey's called Sky.'

'What about the bay?'

'He won't object if you call him Red,' Trant improvised. He held back a grin; he had never called the mule anything he could repeat in front of a child. 'How about you, do you have a name?'

'Sure I do. I'm Jim Blazy. My pa went on to Oregon, him and my brother. They're gonna be back anytime now, Mrs Littleton says so. Mister, do you think we're gonna see Mr Wilkie?'

'I don't rightly know. Why?'

'I didn't like him much, even before he went loco. Lizzie saw him a few days ago. She says he's scarier than the Indians. That's Lizzie, with the fur hat on.' The youngster pointed at the smallest of the children. 'Her ma bought that hat off an Indian, back when it was hot. Lizzie's folks are all dead. Mrs Littleton's looking out for her now.'

'It sounds as if you know everything

that goes on around here, Jim. Did anybody join you folks on the trail in the last month or two?'

'Sure. Mr and Mrs Jewett, and Mr and Mrs Carlotti. They were all at Fort Boise. My pa didn't want them coming along; he said they'd be trouble, what with Mrs Jewett expecting a baby, and Mr Carlotti being sick. Guess he was right, 'cos Mr Carlotti died. Mr Wilkie and Mr Jewett buried him. My pa don't like Mrs Carlotti much, but I do, I think she's real pretty. Lizzy likes her too. She says she wants a dress like that, and she'll wear it all the time and she won't care what Mrs Littleton says. Do you think she's pretty?'

'Of course I do,' Trant replied, aware of the tall woman who strode a little way ahead of them. 'Lizzie doesn't need fancy dresses; she's about the prettiest little girl I ever saw.' Before the boy could set him straight and attempt more embarrassing questions he put another of his own. 'Do you remember meeting up with two men? They'd be riding to Oregon, going the same way as you and your folks. They didn't have a wagon, just a couple of pack horses. One of them is a very big man with a red beard. He'd be hard to miss.'

The boy's brow furrowed as he considered the question. 'No. We met a man with three mules, but he was a goback. He told Pa he was heading home to Missouri. Are you a lawman, mister? Did these men do something bad?'

'No. One of them is a friend of mine. I'm trying to find him, that's all. I think Lizzie's getting tired. Why don't you go and fetch her and tell her she can ride with Tuck for a while.'

Trant pushed the pace, aware of the snow clouds hanging overhead. The women were flagging and he heard them muttering, glancing his way. None of them approached him until after their brief noon break, and then they came in strength, Mrs Littleton in the lead. He was curious to note that the Carlotti woman remained aloof; she kept her place alongside the wagon, talking softly to the child whose turn it was to sit with Tuck.

'We have to stop,' Mrs Littleton said, blocking his way. 'Mrs Jewett is exhausted, being bounced around all these hours.'

'I spoke to Mrs Jewett not ten minutes ago,' Trant replied evenly. 'She wants her daughter to live. The best chance she'll have is if we can reach the Oregon Trail before the snow catches up to us. At least down there we might meet up with some late travellers, or a couple of friendly Indians, or even those menfolk of yours who set off to fetch help. We need food. Up here we can sit and starve and nobody will ever know, not till the spring thaw.'

'Then can't we ride in the wagon?' One woman asked. 'My feet are raw.'

'You're not the only one with sore feet,' Trant said. 'The mule's going short on his near fore. Have you got any idea how far we'd get if those animals can't keep working? We'll stop when the light goes, and not before.' He pushed through them, walking fast to catch up with the wagon. Ahead, Mrs Carlotti half turned, as if she had heard something of the disturbance, the smallest trace of a smile on her face.

Much later, Trant sat by the fire, listening to Tuck's low tuneless whistle from the horse line. Dawn was maybe three hours away. He'd finished his spell of guard duty and he was bone-achingly tired, but the stab wound in his arm had started to trouble him; it should have been tended, but somehow there had never been time. He stood up, setting his back to the fire to let his eyes adjust to the darkness. There was a small stream no more than thirty yards away, perhaps if he let the icy water run over the throbbing flesh it would ease enough to let him rest.

Following the sound of water, Trant made his way to the stream and knelt down, easing his arm out of his coat. The cold bit at him as he pushed up his sleeve; the cloth was stiff with dried blood, and his breath hissed between his lips as skin and flesh tore when he pulled it away. There was ice at the edges of the water, but he plunged his arm into the flow and held it still; the chill hurt far more than the wound.

After a couple of minutes Trant's arm was numb, but the wound was clean. He rocked back on his heels. As he rose, something slammed into the base of his skull and he pitched forward, falling into oblivion.

3

Trant ached with cold; deep shivers shook his whole body. He had to move. If he didn't, the icy numbness invading him would freeze his fingers and toes, moving on up his arms and legs. His heart would slow and then stop: he had to move, or die.

He couldn't lift his head from the ground, and he couldn't recollect where he was, or how he came to be there; opening his eyes revealed nothing. Either he was blind or it was night. Trant made a small sound of frustration as his eyelids slid down again. It would be easy to drift away, to let the cold take him.

There were reasons why he should go on living; he couldn't remember what they were but the knowledge of their existence goaded him to action. Opening his eyes again, he found he could see starlight reflecting on the frozen surface of a stream. He was lying with one hand in the edge of the water. Biting down hard on his lip, he forced the fingers of his hand into a fist. When he opened it again there were shards of ice digging into his palm. Trant put all his ebbing strength into rolling up the gently shelving bank. He curled himself into a ball and lapsed back into unconsciousness.

Time had passed. Somebody was singing in a sweet low voice. He wasn't cold, but lapped in a soft warmth that seemed all of a piece with the music. Trant wondered if this was death, and discovered he no longer cared. He sank into the depths again.

He was moving and the motion puzzled him. What he could feel wasn't the steady rhythmic sway of a horse, or the rattling jolt of a wagon. There was a cold breath of air on his face, yet he was warm. Above him was a grey sky. Turning his head he could see the coarse fibres of the cloth that shrouded him.

Trant began to struggle against the restriction of this cocoon, fighting to free his arms. The motion stopped. Something jarred against his spine and the back of his head and he grunted as the knock reawakened a throbbing pain at the base of his skull.

A face appeared, looking down at him. 'Mrs Carlotti,' he whispered wonderingly.

'Mr Trant.' Her full lips curved in a mocking smile. 'I was beginning to wonder if you would ever wake up. It would have been a pity to put so much effort into towing a dead man.'

'Towing . . . ' he tried to make sense of her words, but it was too much of an effort. She vanished from sight for a moment and returned with a canteen, holding it to his lips. He drank long and deep, and his head began to clear.

'What happened?' he asked.

'Bart Wilkie happened. We woke to find him sitting by the fire, dressed like a scarecrow. Mrs Littleton gave him her husband's old coat to wear, and we all sat down to eat breakfast. It seemed as if he'd forgotten about the raid, and what happened to his daughters. He ordered us to harness the horses and get the wagon moving. There was no sign of you, and when Tuck asked him if he'd seen you he said he hadn't. He said we didn't have time to search, and that you'd probably decided to go on ahead.' She pulled a wry face. 'That's when it all started to fall apart again. When Tuck argued with him, he pulled a gun.'

Trant's hand felt for the holster at his side. 'Mine,' he said.

She nodded. 'Mr Wilkie went crazy again. He screamed at Tuck, but he wasn't making any sense. The children were terrified, and a couple of the women were close to hysterics; I was afraid if they went to pieces he'd start shooting. Since I was closest to the wagon I went looking for a weapon.'

'My rifle was under the seat, along with Tuck's shotgun.'

'I know. They'd gone. Mr Wilkie

must have taken them. He saw me searching though and that took his attention off Tuck so he turned on me. He started calling me names.' She lowered her gaze for a second, and when she looked up the challenge was back in her eyes. 'What he said would have made any lady blush. When Mrs Littleton tried to calm him down he started shouting about me and Paolo Carlotti not being married.'

'I don't understand,' Trant said, shaken as if he had just heard a terrible blasphemy; he wanted this woman to be perfect.

She shrugged. 'Paolo was never interested in women; the only things he loved were the theatre and his whiskey bottle. He wasn't a bad man, but I'd never have married him.'

'But you were travelling together.'

'It's simple enough. We'd set out in a group of eighteen, all singers and musicians travelling together, but then Paolo got sick with the fever. I stayed to nurse him and the rest of them went on. If I hadn't claimed to be Paolo's wife, Mr Littleton wouldn't have taken us along.' Her chin tilted up. 'I wasn't Paolo's wife, but I wasn't his mistress either, no matter what that dirty minded lunatic thought.'

'I don't suppose Wilkie listened to you,' Trant remarked drily. He had freed a hand from the blankets and lifted it to touch the tender spot at the base of his skull. 'The first time I met him he did his best to kill me, and last night he bushwhacked me and tried again. I never even heard him coming.'

'I guessed it was his fault you'd gone missing. When he turned on me I didn't argue, in case he started shooting. He threw me out without so much as a wrap. If Emma Jewett hadn't tossed some food and blankets out of the wagon when they left we'd both have died of cold last night. It was a wonder you'd survived the night before.'

'The night before?' Trant looked up at the sky. 'I came to for a while by the stream, are you saying that was yesterday?'

She nodded. 'It was pure luck Mr Wilkie decided he wasn't going to need the travois.' Her lips curved into a smile again. 'I couldn't get started until I'd warmed you up; you were so cold I was afraid you'd die before I'd got you to the fire. I got going as soon as I could though, and I don't think we're more than three hours behind them. We'll know for sure when we find their campsite. You'd better eat before we move on.'

Trant had managed to free himself from the blankets. He sat up, wincing as pain shot through his head. 'I'll eat while I walk,' he said.

'You need to get your strength back,' she protested.

'What we need is to catch up with Wilkie,' he replied grimly, 'before he loses his head again and shoots somebody.'

* * *

A few small hard flakes of snow started to fall as the light waned. Trant had walked in silence for hours, resisting the urge to lie down and sleep. Pain throbbed through his head. Behind him the woman dragged the travois, as silent as he, and as resolute.

When Trant could no longer see the ground beneath his feet and each stride was a desperate stumble, he obeyed her pull on his arm and stopped. With the travois propped up against the rock to give them shelter from the wind and the occasional flurry of snow, they ate, as they had walked, in silence, and then Trant gratefully let sleep take him, lying on the bare rock with his arm for a pillow.

Perhaps it was the singing that woke him, though her voice was so low he could barely hear it. His head was cushioned on something soft, and he was beautifully warm, just as he'd been when he'd half woken the night before. Stirring, he felt the generous curve of her figure fold more firmly round him;

his head lay against her shoulder; she had wrapped them together in the blankets.

'Go back to sleep,' she said softly.

'Seems an awful waste,' he muttered, sinking obediently into slumber again. Whether his words reached her ears he couldn't tell, but he thought he heard her laugh. Some hours later he woke fully; it was still dark, but she was no longer curled against him. Trant sat up in alarm.

'I'm here,' she said, ducking back into the shelter, bringing cold air with her. 'I thought the snow might have made it light enough to go on, but it hasn't covered the ground.'

She crept in beside him and tried to take him in her arms again, apparently unembarrassed. Trant shrank away a little, too wakeful now to ignore her nearness.

'If you don't stay under the blankets we'll both freeze,' she said calmly. 'I have a rock close at hand, just in case you try anything.'

Trant grinned into the darkness, trying to pretend her nearness had no effect on him. 'I'd rather you didn't hit me, Wilkie was enough. Besides, I could never take advantage of a woman who hadn't been properly introduced. I don't even know your name. I only know you're not really Mrs Carlotti. And I think it's time you told me why you're trekking across America dressed in satin and lace.'

She laughed. 'I'll swap my story for yours,' she replied. 'You act like a frontiersman half the time, then you forget and talk like a real eastern gentleman.'

'That's no mystery. My father was a very wealthy man, and as a child I lacked for nothing. When I turned twenty I got tired of being pampered and started living life the way I chose. I've tried my hand at quite a few things since then. Take your pick, ma'am, cowboy, soldier, newspaper reporter, fur trader or gold prospector. I even spent a spell as a lumberjack.'

'And who among so many is the real Mr Trant?'

'I've no idea. But my friends call me Adam.'

'Adam,' she repeated obediently, a trace of humour in her voice. 'Oh my. What a very good thing my mother resisted the temptation to christen me Eve.'

It was his turn to laugh. 'I'd say it's a downright shame.'

'That's enough. I suspect you have more to tell, but I'll let that pass for the moment. My story won't take long. My name is Ann Geary, and I set out for Oregon with several gowns at least as grand as this poor thing. I'm a singer; I can't afford to look drab amongst all that gilt and velvet they use in the theatre. I'm not in the habit of wearing my stage clothes during the day, but Emma Jewett had asked me to give a performance and I got changed as we stopped to camp for the night. Since my wagon was at the back of the line it was the first to be attacked. If Mr Blazy hadn't come along and pulled me onto his horse I would probably have been killed. All my other clothes were burnt to cinders, but I could hardly make a fuss, not when people had been killed, and two young girls were missing. And poor Sam Jewett was badly hurt.'

'You and Mrs Jewett are good friends.' Trant observed.

'We travelled to Fort Boise with the same wagon train, and we both joined the Littletons' train there. Although she knew Paolo was my manager, not my husband, she kept my secret, and when she was widowed I did what I could to comfort her.'

'Do you have any family? Is there somebody waiting for you in Oregon?' Trant asked.

'There's nobody waiting for me anywhere,' she replied. 'I never knew my father. My mother kept food on the table by teaching music, and she always believed my voice was good enough for the stage. For as long as she could she trained me, but by the time I was sixteen she was very sick. When she knew she hadn't much longer to live she asked her old friend Paolo Carlotti to take care of me. He kept his promise, until the day he died.'

There was a brief silence. 'Will you sing for me?' Trant asked tentatively.

'I sang for you last night,' she said. 'It's not my fault if you didn't hear the performance.'

'I did, just for a moment. When I heard you singing I thought I was dead, and you were an angel.'

She laughed again, and began softly singing the lullaby he recalled from the night before.

One song melted easily into another; Trant felt her every breath. He was more than halfway to losing his heart to Ann Geary; he had told no lie when he assured her she was safe lying here against him, but not because he wasn't tempted. At another time, in some other place, it might be different. His thoughts drifted, and it was as if the icy wind had blown into their warm haven.

Drowning out the song, another woman's words echoed in the back of his mind. Until he could find some way to silence their rebuke he'd have no peace.

When at last Ann's lovely voice faded into silence, Trant stirred, pulling away from her. 'I think it's light enough to see our way,' he said.

He crawled out from behind the travois, straightening to find that they were no longer alone. A few feet away stood a figure from a nightmare. John Littleton's coat, hanging loose on Wilkie's wasted frame, was thickly crusted with blood. Red stains spattered the man's bare feet; even his hair and face were streaked with red. He had a gory knife in one hand, while in the other he held a lump of bloody flesh.

4

Trant had no weapon, and only a second in which to save both their lives. He grabbed the travois and swung it in front of him. Wilkie kept coming, sweeping the wooden poles aside as if they were twigs; he had the abnormal strength of the insane, caring nothing for the damage he might do to himself, intent only on reaching Trant.

Summoning his own dwindling reserves and well aware that he wasn't at his best, thanks to the lunatic's previous attack, Trant felt the shock of the blow running up his arms. The layers of canvas absorbed much of its power, although the blade sliced through them and barely missed his body. Slamming his makeshift shield at Wilkie's face, Trant felt another impact as the knife bedded itself in the frame of the travois, and thrust it away.

Unwilling to let go of the knife, but unable to pull it free, Wilkie went down under Trant's onslaught.

Glancing round, Trant saw that Ann Geary had retreated a little way up the trail. 'Get out of here,' he shouted. 'Run!' There was no time to see if she had obeyed. Wilkie was tugging at the hilt and the blade was about to come free. He had to be disarmed; even without a weapon he was a formidable opponent. Trant steeled himself, watching the wildly circling blade, wondering if he could duck beneath it and get past the madman's guard.

'Mr Wilkie!' The sound brought a flicker of awareness to the lunatic's eyes, and for a heartbeat he was still. 'I've seen Katherine and Jane,' Ann Geary went on. 'Your daughters, Mr Wilkie, they're looking for you.'

Wilkie paused, swinging round to face her. She had discarded the blanket and loosed her hair, and she stood before him in all the magnificence of her shabby finery.

‘Whore!’ he roared. ‘Liar!’

‘I’m not lying,’ she said calmly, standing her ground. ‘And I’m not a whore. Your daughters need you, Mr Wilkie; they want me to take you to them. Come on, it’s this way.’ Shaking his head like a bull tormented by a fly, Wilkie took a step in her direction. ‘I sent the others to God,’ he screeched, ‘but there’s no refuge for a wanton. You have to go back to the hell you came from.’ Even as he spoke he lunged at her, but Trant was faster; his fists bunched together, he landed a swinging blow on the side of the man’s head. They went down together; as Trant’s full weight fell on the smaller man he distinctly heard the crack of bone.

With a howl of rage and a power that should have been far beyond his depleted and abused body, Wilkie somehow threw Trant aside. The knife was still in his fist, although his hand hung at an impossible angle; his arm was broken, but he seemed unaware of it.

The woman had picked up the ruins of the travois, and suddenly she was there, at Wilkie's back, tall and erect, an Amazon come to battle. She beat the poles at Wilkie's damaged arm, and the knife dropped to the ground.

Trant rose to his feet, his breath labouring. Roaring a challenge, for that brief moment as far beyond sense as the man before him, he careered into Wilkie, bearing him bodily back a dozen head-long paces until he was smashed into the rock where they had sheltered overnight.

Wilkie slumped, dropping forward against Trant, his head lolling. The crazy light went from his eyes as one last breath rattled in his chest. His own fury forgotten, Trant caught the lifeless body and lowered it to the ground.

Ann came to him, putting her arms round his neck, and kissing him on the lips. The world reeled. He would have given a great deal to lose himself in her embrace, but he pulled away. 'We have to go and see what happened down there,' he said wearily. 'What did he say? He'd sent them to God? Sweet Jesu.'

'*We're* still alive, Adam, there's a chance some of them escaped.'

He nodded without much conviction, feeling sick to his core, wondering what the madman might have done to Emma Jewett and her baby, trapped in the wagon. And there were the other children . . .

Trant bent to feel among the folds of the coat Wilkie wore, straightening with a revolver in his hand. It was his own gun, still loaded. If Wilkie had thought to use that instead of the knife they'd have had no chance. He offered the weapon to Ann Geary. 'You'd better take this. I'll go on ahead.'

She pushed the revolver resolutely back at him. 'We'll go together.'

A quarter of a mile down the trail they found a woman lying face down, her arms flung wide, one single stab wound to her back.

'It's Cecilia Pross,' Ann said, as Trant

bent over the body.

'There's nothing we can do,' Trant said, rising and turning away. 'The blow was straight to the heart, she must have died quickly.'

'We're just going to leave her here?'

'She's not going to care.'

Her chin came up, and then dropped. She nodded and her hand crept into his.

At first glance the campsite looked deserted, the wagon drawn up to one side, the embers of a fire smouldering nearby. The smell of death hung heavy in the air. Going closer, Trant discovered why. The mule lay with its throat cut and half its hide stripped away; it looked as if Wilkie had started to butcher it.

'Here,' Ann said softly, her tone bringing him back to the wagon. Two women lay side by side beneath it, still wrapped in their blankets as if they slept. Like Cecilia Pross, each had been killed with a single stab wound, aimed accurately at the heart.

'This was his idea of mercy,' Trant said bitterly.

'They didn't have a chance. Emma . . . ' Ann whispered. There were tears coursing silently down her face as she made to open the canvas hanging. Trant pushed her to one side and lifted the flap. A pair of pale blue eyes stared at him, huge in the girl's white face. She clutched the baby tighter to her, and it let out a lusty yell.

'Emma?' Ann Geary climbed into the wagon to embrace her friend, both of them weeping openly.

'He pulled back the curtain and stood looking at me,' the girl sobbed. 'I thought he was going to kill me, but he went away. I think it must have been because of Dawn.' She looked down at the child in her arms, and more tears came.

Trant left the two women together and resumed his search. It took him several minutes to find Tuck. He must have lured Wilkie away from the wagon, fighting for his life every step of the way; his blood had left long smears in the dust. There had been no single killing blow for his friend. Trant bent to close the staring eyes, long since glazed and sightless.

'I heard it. He saved the children, he shouted at them to run.' Emma Jewett had come, clinging to Ann for support. She pointed up a rock-strewn slope. 'They went up there. By the time he'd killed Tuck, Mr Wilkie seemed to forget about them. Mrs Littleton ran off too.'

'Do you know what happened to the horses?' Trant asked.

'Tuck turned them loose. I guess he thought Mr Wilkie would butcher them.'

Trant nodded, his face bleak. There was a chance the grey would come to his call, if it hadn't wandered too far. 'So with luck we've still got a way out of here. I'll look for the children first.'

Ann stopped him, putting a hand on his arm. 'Adam, how are we going to bury them? We can't just leave them, but the ground's so hard . . . '

'See if you can find a cave, or just a place where there's space under a rock. You can put them all together and pile stones over the top. But you'll have to be quick, we need to move on. If I can't catch the horses it's going to be a long walk.'

Trant found the children almost a mile from the camp, cold and scared but unharmed, all huddled under one blanket. Jim Blazy told him they'd seen Mrs Littleton, but that she hadn't seemed to hear when he called out to her. 'She was over that way, sitting on the ground, sort of rocking herself. I didn't want to holler too loud,' he added earnestly, 'in case Mr Wilkie heard me. He was just plain loco.'

Mrs Littleton had stopped rocking, though she was shivering violently with the cold. When Trant told her to take the children back to the wagon the woman rose obediently.

'You don't need to worry about Wilkie, he's gone for good this time,' Trant said. 'I'll be along in a while; I have to catch the horses.'

Mrs Littleton nodded, lifting little Lizzie into her arms, still without uttering a word.

'Can I come and help?' Jim Blazy asked. 'I think I know where they'll be. I rode up here with my brother, Shad. The grazing is real good over that-away, we took all the horses up there for the night.'

* * *

Day followed day, and the snow held off, though the temperature dipped and all the streams froze. To keep the weight down now they were without the mule, Emma Jewett drove the two horse team, while Trant and Ann carried the younger children by turns. Mrs Littleton performed whatever tasks she was set in silence, and took care of little Lizzie; the woman hadn't spoken a word since the day of the massacre.

'Look there.' Trant pointed at a fold in the hills. 'By nightfall we'll be back on the Oregon Trail. Even this late in the year there's a good chance we'll meet up with somebody soon. We might be able to buy fresh horses, and maybe a shotgun.'

'I'd settle for some fresh food,' Ann said, halting at his side. 'Adam, shouldn't we go to Fort Boise? Why are you so set on getting to Oregon?'

He gave her no direct answer. 'I wasted over a month already.' He turned to her, his face suddenly hard. 'I'm heading for Oregon. Anybody who'd rather go back east can join up with the first company we meet.'

It was mid afternoon when Jim Blazy, walking a little ahead of the wagon, began shouting and leaping up and down on the spot in excitement. 'Look there!'

A long column was winding its way eastwards along the Oregon Trail. At the front were men on horseback, followed by many more on foot, with wagons bringing up the rear.

'I counted the wagons,' Jim said as

Trant came to stand beside him, 'six of 'em.'

'Looks like the army,' Trant said. 'See that, Mrs Littleton? You couldn't have a better escort. I just hope there's somebody with a spare shotgun and a couple of horses to sell.' He drew his revolver and fired three shots into the air. Jim began to jump up and down again, waving his arms wildly.

'They heard! They've seen us.'

Two horsemen were peeling away, riding fast. Ann came to stand beside Trant, watching them come. She returned his smile, but there was a troubled look in her eyes. As the riders approached, Jim Blazy gave a shout of joy and sprinted to meet them; one was a young man who wasn't in uniform. He leant down and scooped the boy to the front of his saddle; even at a distance the similarity between the two brothers was striking, and they rode in with identical wide smiles. 'This is my brother Shad,' Jim yelled, 'Pa's in one of the wagons.'

'Captain Orslow,' the other man introduced himself and looked around. 'I gather you're members of the Littleton party; I was expecting to see a much larger group.'

'This is it,' Trant replied flatly, offering his hand. 'I'm Adam Trant; I found these folks stranded in the mountains.' He named the other survivors, remembering to introduce Ann as Mrs Carlotti. The captain's eyes widened at the sight of her bedraggled finery.

'Is your troop on the way to Fort Boise?' Trant asked.

'Yes, but we won't be staying long,' the man replied, switching his attention reluctantly back to Trant. 'We're ordered further east.'

'Even so, I'd be obliged if you'd take Mrs Littleton with you, and any of the others who want to head that way,' Trant said.

'I'm sure the major won't have any objection,' Captain Orslow said. 'We'll be calling a halt for the night soon, you can ask him yourself.'

'I'll do that. And if you don't mind, we'll save telling our story,' he jerked his head back towards the three women, who had congregated around Shad Blazy. 'Going over it more than once would be hard on them.'

Orslow's gaze flicked over the travellers again. 'I'll explain the situation to the major; I'm sure he'll agree to an early halt,' he said. 'If you want I could fetch some troopers to give you a hand.'

'We can manage,' Trant assured him, 'but a good meal would be welcome once we join you, along with a change of team in the morning.' He half turned, wondering if Ann could hear what he was saying. 'And I'll be needing to buy a saddle and some gear, maybe a pack mule. I have to get to Oregon, and I've got a lot of lost time to make up.'

'We've a sutler who'll be happy to oblige, though I won't vouch for his prices,' the captain said. 'I'd better head back.' With a sketchy salute he remounted and put spurs to his horse.

5

Major Whitethorn was a tall spare man, sparing too with his words; he listened without interrupting as Emma Jewett and Ann Geary related the history of the Littletons' wagon train since it left Fort Boise two months before. Mrs Littleton sat with the other women but although she seemed to be following the conversation she never said a word. When the major asked, Trant filled in his share of the story. Ann had made no mention of her part in his final fight with Wilkie, and he saw no need to disclose any details.

There was silence when the tale came to an end. Major Whitethorn cleared his throat. 'A tragedy,' he said, 'I'm sorry for your losses. These so-called white Indians have been active in other places along the trail, that's why we're here. Captain, perhaps you'd care to explain.'

'Of course sir.' He turned to Trant. 'We know a little about these marauders. It's the first time they've attacked so far west; we wouldn't expect to hear of them venturing onto the Fullerton cut-off. That particular short cut was a failure from the start; the only party to reach Oregon by that route took over seven months, and they lost more than half their number in the process.'

'I gathered from Tuck that somebody they met at South Pass persuaded Littleton to try it,' Trant said. 'According to them it was at least a week shorter than the old trail.'

'A deliberate and cold-blooded trap,' Orslow nodded, 'and it's not the first time. We have information that these raiders have a base not far to the east of Fort Boise. They're led by a renegade by the name of Hammer; we've been sent to track him down. He commands a force of almost a hundred men, and I'm raising a volunteer force to add to the unit's strength, Mr Trant; over seventy emigrants and Oregonians have already enrolled, all of them committed to putting an end to these raids. I'm hoping you'll join us.'

Trant shook his head. 'I'm sorry, I have urgent business elsewhere. I need to get to Oregon as soon as possible.'

'A few weeks, that's all we're asking.' Major Whitethorn urged. 'You've seen what these men are capable of; surely you want to prevent more of these massacres.'

'A man of your resourcefulness would be of great use to me,' the captain added. 'The volunteers are all itching to fight, but I'm short of men who can issue orders and command respect. If you volunteered to join us I wouldn't hesitate to put you in charge of a platoon.'

'As I said, I'm sorry. If the circumstances were different I'd be happy to accept your offer,' Trant replied, 'but I'm trying to find two men who left Kanesville just three days before me and time's running out. I've faced so many delays that I guess they must be in Oregon by now. It's a big territory. If I can't get through until the spring I may never trace them.'

'Yet you followed the Littletons' train on the Fullerton cut-off.'

Trant shrugged. 'I was led astray, though not quite the same way as they were. Once I caught up with them I couldn't leave women and children stranded in the mountains, but now they are safe I have to move on.'

'If I may ask, Mr Trant, what business do you have with the men you're after?' Whitethorn asked. 'Are you a peace officer?'

'No, my business is strictly personal,' Trant replied. He could feel all their eyes on him, knowing they were reading a threat in his words, but were unwilling to say any more.

'These men, do you know their names?' Captain Orslow put in. 'Could be we've come across them. You never know, they might even be amongst our volunteers.'

'The older one is called Davie Gaunt.

He's a big man, over six foot three and broad with it, maybe forty years old and bald as a coot. Most people call him Red, because of the colour of his beard. He usually rides a paint horse, the sort the Indians are so keen on, but a lot bigger.'

Across the fire, Emma Jewett let out a little gasp, her face pale. 'But I've seen that man, just the way you describe him! His horse has a crooked blaze that runs down from one ear to the opposite side of its nose.'

'That's right!' Trant leant forward, hardly able to believe what he was hearing. 'Where did you see him?' he demanded.

'He was on the raid,' she said breathlessly. 'He and a couple of Indians rode off with our horses.'

'Do I gather this man is a friend of yours, Trant?' the major barked.

'I rode with him for a while up in Canada,' Trant said, 'I guess I'd have called him a friend. Davie's not beyond a little dishonesty, but I'd never have thought he was capable of murder.' He shook his head. 'Maybe I was wrong about him. Please, Mrs Jewett, did you see another white man riding with him? He'd be young, about five feet eight and skinny, less than half Red's size. He has very fair hair and grey eyes.'

She shook her head. 'No. The other men I saw both had black hair. I'm certain they were Indians.'

'I think maybe you should explain your reasons for — ' Whitethorn began, but Trant had already turned to Orslow.

'With your permission, Captain, I'd like to change my mind and join your volunteers.'

* * *

With a fresh team of horses, the Blazy wagon was deemed fit to carry Mrs Jewett and Mrs Carlotti to Fort Boise, while room was made for Mrs Littleton and the children to travel in one of the supply wagons.

Trant rode the grey near the head of

the column, alongside Captain Orslow. Unlike Major Whitethorn, the captain seemed unconcerned about Trant's connection with one of the marauders; he thought it might prove useful in the hunt for the white Indians.

'You believed this man Red was going to Oregon, but perhaps he had other plans,' Orslow suggested. 'Did he ever mention having ridden with the Paiutes or the Chinooks?'

'It's not something we talked about,' Trant replied. 'I don't think I can help you, Captain. To the best of my knowledge Davie Gaunt was intending to ride all the way to Oregon. He was travelling with a man called Sim Morrow, and he'd mentioned the Fullerton cut-off. I don't recall anything else that could be of use. He told me he intended to head south in the spring, maybe take a ship down the coast to California.'

'This other man then,' Orslow persisted, 'had he ever been in this territory before?'

'No, he'd lived all his life in Iowa. If the two men have split up it's possible he'd have made his way back there,' Trant said. Even as he spoke, he knew his words were untrue. Sim Morrow had good reason never to return to Iowa, thanks to his last meeting with Trant. 'With your permission, Captain, I'd like to ride back and see how my friends are getting along.'

If Trant had been deliberately avoiding Ann's company he didn't admit it to himself. He halted the grey and sat watching the column pass by. When the little wagon came alongside he didn't immediately recognize the woman who sat holding the reins beside Emma Jewett; Ann had finally obtained a change of clothes. She wore a black dress, as befitted her status as a widow, with a dark shawl wrapped around her shoulders, and she had her hair completely hidden under a sober bonnet.

'Good day to you, Mr Trant,' she greeted him. 'I thought perhaps you'd grown tired of my company.'

'Good day, Mrs Carlotti,' he responded, ignoring her jibe. 'If Mrs Jewett wouldn't mind driving that rig for a while, I'd be grateful if you'd take a walk with me.'

They drew aside from the train, easily keeping pace with the slow moving supply wagons, most of them hauled by yoke of oxen. For a long time Trant didn't speak, his thoughts far away. At length the woman halted, laying a hand on his arm. 'Tell me, Adam,' she said gently, 'I know there was something you weren't prepared to admit to the major. Who are those men you're looking for? What's important enough to bring you so far?'

Still he didn't speak. He turned and walked on, his silence like a solid wall between them. She followed him, her expression bleak.

'Very well, if you won't talk then I shall. I love you, Adam. I've never said those words to a man before, but with you, for good or ill, I can't help myself. And I need to know if there's any future for us. If you have no feelings for me — '

'You know I do,' he said forcefully. 'But I can't make promises. I have to see this thing through first.'

'Are you married?' She shot the question at him, doing her best to hide her anguish.

No.' His denial came quick and vehement and she nodded, believing him, but the pain was still there in her eyes.

'Do you have to kill these men?' she asked, a slight tremble in her voice. 'I saw you fight Wilkie, remember. I don't think murder would come easily to you, Adam.'

'Please.' He turned, taking her in his arms. 'I can't share this with anyone, not even you. Maybe if I can put things right, it will be different. I'll say it this once, Ann, but never again until this is over. I love you. And I don't recall that I ever said that before either.' He resisted the temptation to kiss her and almost thrust her away from him.

Lifting into the saddle he galloped away, leaving her staring after him.

The next day, Trant was at the head of the column once again, when they spotted a small party of horsemen coming towards them, each leading a pack mule. 'We sent a messenger ahead,' Captain Orslow said. 'Could be we have some more volunteers.'

'Only if they were too impatient to wait for you to reach Fort Boise,' Trant pointed out. 'I'm wondering if Mr Littleton made it to safety after all.' He turned, beckoning to Shad Blazy. By the time the youngster joined them the oncoming riders could be seen quite clearly. 'Anybody there you recognize?'

John Littleton was a big man, florid of face and possessing a great opinion of himself. He listened with some impatience as Captain Orslow related the disasters that had overcome his party. This news was met with the assertion that they should have remained safe in the cave where he himself had installed them. 'As you can see, I have organized relief. With these men I've hired, I could have reached them long before the snow.'

'They only had food enough for a week when I found them,' Trant pointed out. 'That would have run out by now. Even with what I was carrying we barely had enough to get us back on the Oregon Trail.'

Littleton shook his large head. 'It's a shame a man can't be in two places at once,' he said, giving Trant a dismissive look. 'Perhaps you'd escort me to my wife, Captain.'

'Mr Trant will do that, sir,' Orslow replied, giving the man a smart salute. 'I have to return to my duties.'

'Didn't two of you head for Fort Boise?' Trant asked, as they rode back past the column.

'Pross died,' Littleton replied shortly.

'That'll be hard news for his little brother and sister to hear,' Trant said, 'especially since they lost their mother.'

There was no more conversation between them. Their arrival at the supply train coincided with the noon halt, and they found Mrs Littleton stooped over a box at the rear of the wagon, the children grouped around her. Straightening, she saw her husband climb down from the saddle. As he walked towards her the woman dropped to the ground in a dead faint.

6

'Our mounted force will be leaving at first light, all men to be issued with rations for eight days,' Major Whitethorn said. He jabbed a finger at the hand drawn map on the table. 'Captain Orslow, your volunteers will take the eastern route, and cut off any escape in that direction. Our information puts Hammer in this area, so our main attack will be made from here, driving directly north. The supply train will set up a base at this point.'

Trant was only half listening, his mind on the men he hoped to find before the attack started. If Davie Gaunt and Sim Morrow were among Hammer's marauders, once they were on the opposing side in a pitched battle, he would have no hope of tracking them down.

With the briefing over Trant was kept

too busy to think of anything but the task in hand; Orslow was right, few of the volunteers were accustomed to the responsibility of command. What he hadn't mentioned was that even fewer of them were accustomed to taking orders. By the time he had the men lined up to check their arms, Trant was already working on a short fuse.

'You tryin' to tell me this gun ain't no use, mister?' a mountain man pushed his face aggressively close to Trant's, wagging a finger under his nose. 'I killed me a grizzly with it, only last week.'

'But we have no ammunition for it,' Trant said. 'And you only have two rounds left.'

'That ain't no fault of mine. We was told we'd be given what we needed.'

'Exactly. An army issue carbine, along with fifty rounds.' Trant waved the man towards Shad Blazy, who was handing out the weapons. 'Take it and move on.'

'An' if I don't?' The man spat at

Trant's feet. 'What you gonna do about it?'

'This.' Quick as a snake, Trant struck, his right fist planting a solid blow on the man's jaw. As he reeled, Trant's left came across to black his eye. Recovering quickly, the mountain man lunged forward, only to come to a dead stop as the muzzle of Trant's revolver ground against his neck, the click of the hammer loud in the sudden silence.

'We're here to fight these marauders and stop the raids on the Oregon Trail,' Trant said. 'Once that's done you can take a swing at me, but right now I've been given a job to do, and you're getting in the way. Pick up the carbine.'

'Something wrong, Mr Trant?' Captain Orslow pushed his way through the waiting line of men.

'Not that I know of, Captain,' Trant replied calmly, keeping the gun pressed into the man's tangled beard.

'He blacked my eye,' the mountain man protested.

Orslow inspected the damage with a

show of interest. He nodded. 'I'd say he made a good job of it, but if you're not satisfied I'll gladly black the other one for you.'

The laughter from the rest of the volunteers put an end to the man's rebellion. He accepted the carbine from Blazy and stomped away. From then on things went more smoothly, but it was dark by the time they were finished. Trant helped the youngster pack the remaining guns and ammunition. 'Return these to the stores as well,' he ordered, handing Blazy the sheets of paper he'd used to record what had been issued, 'then you're done for the day.'

'Yes sir. Can I ask you something, Mr Trant? It's about Jane Wilkie. I wanted to talk to Captain Orslow, but there's been no time. Maybe you could help.'

Stifling a yawn, Trant took a moment to work out what the youngster was talking about. 'Jane Wilkie? Wasn't she one of the girls taken by the marauders?'

'Yes sir. It's just, the way everyone's talking, we'll charge into that camp with every gun blazing. But suppose Jane and Katherine are there? What if they're still alive?'

Trant shook his head, searching for some kind of answer that wouldn't be too hard on the boy. 'I'm sorry if you were sweet on the girl, son. Men like these . . . ' Apart from the damage they'd done to the Littleton party, he'd learnt from Orslow about other atrocities committed by the white Indians, but he had no intention of sharing such horrors with young Blazy. He had no doubt the two girls had died long ago, and maybe been glad of it. 'You have to face it, boy, she's gone, as sure as if she was buried with her father.'

'But what if you're wrong?' Shad demanded desperately. 'If there's just a chance, isn't there something we can do?'

'Like what?'

'I don't know. I thought of riding on ahead, maybe seeing if there's any way to talk to this man Hammer.' He hefted the rifle in his hand. 'This is a good gun, and there's my horse, maybe I could do a trade.'

'They'd shoot you before you got close and help themselves to your gun and horse. I wouldn't be surprised if they took your scalp too,' Trant said. 'There's not a chance in ten thousand that she's survived, Shad. Don't waste time thinking about what can't be, just keep your mind on settling the score.'

Silence was falling over the camp as Trant approached the cabin he was sharing with a dozen other volunteers. He reached a hand to the latch, his thoughts focused on nothing more challenging than his bedroll. A voice from the darkness stopped him in his tracks.

'You kept me waiting a long time.' She was standing in the shadows to the side of the hut. Trant spun round to face her.

'Mrs Carlotti. You shouldn't be out here at this hour.'

'Is that all you've got to say to me, Adam?' She came to him, her expression unreadable. 'You don't need to worry, I'm not here to make things difficult for you. I came because of Mrs Littleton.'

'Mrs Littleton?' He stared at her in confusion. 'I don't understand.'

'There's something she wanted you to know before you left,' the woman replied.

'If she has information about the marauders she should have told the captain.'

'And that would have saved you the embarrassment of talking to me,' she said, a sad smile on her lips. 'I'm sorry. This won't take long. Since her husband came back Mrs Littleton has started talking again. She gave Mr Wilkie that knife; he told her he needed it to butcher some meat. She'd convinced herself that he had recovered. Ever since, she's been blaming herself for what happened.'

'He could have used my gun and

killed every one of us,' Trant said bleakly. 'The man was crazy, you can tell her it made no difference.'

'I already did. But that's not all. She saw a young man with fair hair riding with the raiders. He wasn't with the men who took the horses, he was attacking the wagons.'

Trant digested this news in silence for a few moments, and then sighed. 'Thank her for me. If it was him — ' he broke off. 'You shouldn't be here, I'll walk you back.'

'There's no need.' She lifted a tentative hand and laid it against his cheek. 'Good luck, Adam, take care of yourself.' She whisked away into the night.

* * *

Adam Trant lay on a tilting slab of rock, snaking his way up towards the top. If he'd guessed right, the marauders' camp lay almost directly below him; he'd been surprised to get this far without running into any lookouts.

It hadn't been easy to get away from Orslow and the other volunteers, but he'd finally persuaded the captain to allow him to ride ahead to make a brief reconnaissance, promising to return within two hours to report. He was very much overdue; there would be riders out looking for him. His horse was well hidden, but time wasn't on his side.

A deep fissure appeared in the rock to his right, a dry gully that had once carried water but was now filled with a jumble of broken rock. Trant slithered down towards it. The shadows would hide him — he would be less visible there than on the bare slope above. He just had to be careful; if he dislodged a stone he could easily alert the men below.

Gradually the opposite side of the canyon came into view. Trant ducked his head and froze; there was a man posted almost directly across from him, perched on a rock with a rifle in his hands. After waiting several long moments, Trant lifted his gaze. The man was giving his full attention to the entrance of the gorge, to the south. Inching forward again, Trant came to rest in the shadows at the mouth of the gully; from here he could survey the scene below with little chance of being seen.

The raiders had built themselves a sizeable encampment, with a cluster of shacks leaning against the far wall of the canyon. A great many horses and mules were corralled at the further end. Trant narrowed his eyes, studying the hillside above the enclosure. He couldn't be sure, but it looked as if there might be a way out to the north. Somehow he doubted if a man like Hammer would allow himself to be trapped in a dead end.

Apart from the man keeping watch there was nobody in sight. Trant eased himself a hazardous six inches closer to the long drop below, so he could look straight down; there was more activity on this side of the canyon. Along with a cluster of Indian tepees it seemed there was a cave dug into the cliff. Men came and went, helping themselves to coffee from a pot over a fire. Outside the cave two men sat playing cards, watched by a third. This was a big man, dwarfing the others; he removed his hat briefly, baring his bald head and revealing his bushy red beard: it was unmistakably Davie Gaunt. Two cold and weary hours later, Trant eased his stiffening body out of the confines of the gully, keeping low until he was well away from the skyline. He had seen one man who might have been Sim Morrow, but he was far from sure.

It would soon be dark. Trant had come up with a plan of sorts; all he needed was luck. He had to reach Red Gaunt, and hope his previous acquaintance with the man would be enough to protect him from the rest of the gang. As for Morrow, it was probably best not to think about what might happen if they met down there among the white Indians. Trant wanted that encounter to be on his own terms.

Coming down towards his horse, standing tethered to a dead tree stump, Trant came to a sudden halt. There was a second animal, tied alongside his own. He put a hand to the butt of his gun, treading softly, alert for the faintest sound. The brief chink of falling rock made him turn. Somebody was coming down the hill, no more than twenty yards from where he had descended. It was Shad Blazy.

'Mr Trant, did you see her?' The youngster came across to him at a run, feet slipping on the rock, within a hairsbreadth of losing his balance, his eyes alight with some powerful emotion. 'I was pretty sure, but if you saw her too — '

'Didn't I tell you — ?' Trant began, angry that the youth had followed him.

'But she was there, Jane. Didn't you see her? You had a better spot than me, you must have been able to see pretty much the whole of the camp. There was a girl by the cave, I'm sure of it.'

'I didn't see her,' Trant said, but even as he spoke he doubted his words. Thinking back, there had been somebody. He'd seen a flash of pale clothing, something that didn't belong down in the marauder's camp among all those men, but he'd been tied up in trying to locate Sim Morrow. 'There could have been a woman, but that doesn't mean anything. Look, kid, I told you before, those girls are dead. It's hard, but that's the way it is.'

'No!' Shad faced him, a fiery certainty on his face. 'I tell you I saw her. It was Jane. I'm going down there, as soon as it's dark.'

'You won't get halfway. They've got guards posted, and there are Indians in those tepees, real ones. They'd smell you coming.'

'There's a track in from the north.' The boy said, moving past Trant and heading down to the horses. 'I could see it clear as anything. If I can get to the top of it before dark I'll sneak down and try to find her. Once the army comes those men'll kill her, I know it.'

Trant followed him, putting a hand on the horse's rein as the youngster lifted into the saddle. 'Listen, you'll have no chance. There's no point you getting yourself killed. There's another way we can do this.'

'We?' the boy's voice cracked in his excitement. 'You mean you'll help me? Are we going in through the canyon?'

'We aren't doing anything. If you stop acting dumb and do as you're told, I might be able to find out about that girl, maybe even bring her back. I've got business of my own with a man in that camp, and it's possible I can get amongst those people without getting my head blown off. Meantime, you're going to take the captain a message from me. He needs to know what we've seen. You have to tell him there's no way out of the canyon this side, not for a man on horseback. It's a waste of time him plugging an imaginary gap to the east if he leaves the north open.'

'How come you know those men?'

the boy asked suspiciously, trying to free his rein from Trant's grip. 'A bunch of killers . . . '

'I said I knew one man, not the whole bunch. Besides, knowing a bad man doesn't make you the same as him,' Trant replied. 'Come on, I'll tell you a bit about Davie Gaunt while we ride. Before I go I need you to give me your word you'll ride straight back to Captain Orslow.'

The boy looked about as willing as a mule.

Trant sighed. 'Would I be sending for the army if I was in cahoots with the gang?'

'Could be you'll go and warn them to run while they can.'

'If I was planning to do that I'd be pretty damn stupid sending you for help instead of knocking you on your fool head and leaving you for the crows! Come on, kid, we're wasting time.'

7

With every sense telling him to turn tail and run, Trant kept the grey to a measured jog. The feeling of being watched had lain heavy on him for the last half mile. There were a hundred places where lookouts might be posted, but he resisted the temptation to look for them. He kept his gaze fixed on the way ahead as if he knew no fear, trying to ignore the itch between his shoulder blades.

As far as he could judge, he was about halfway to the raiders' camp. He could turn around now, set spurs to the grey's flanks and probably make it out of this narrowing valley alive; there were scattered trees and the light was poor, not ideal conditions for shooting at a moving target. But Davie Gaunt was ahead of him; maybe Sim Morrow was there too. If he turned back now, both men might soon be dead, and he would have lost his last chance to rid himself of the burden he'd carried for so long.

He tried not to think of the woman he'd left behind in Fort Boise; if he didn't finish what he'd set out to do, he'd never be the sort of man she deserved.

Movement high on the eastern cliff caught Trant's eye, the glint of metal picked out by the last of the light. He didn't alter his pace. If the marauders had wind of the planned attack he was already a dead man; even if they didn't, his plan was crazy. He turned his thoughts resolutely to the girl Shad Blazy claimed to have seen. The youngster had left him with great reluctance, finally persuaded to carry the message to the captain when Trant swore he wouldn't leave the marauders' camp without attempting to rescue the girl.

Something ploughed up the dirt before the grey's hoofs, and a second later the sound of the shot reached

Trant's ears, the echo ricocheting around the valley. Trant soothed the grey, bringing it to a halt. He looked around, trying to see where the bullet had come from, keeping his hands well away from his weapons.

'Stay there,' a man shouted. Trant obeyed; he didn't have long to wait. Three men appeared from the gloom before him, riding hard. They pulled up in a flurry of dirt, one on each side of him, the third blocking his path.

The man to Trant's right was young and fair, only a faint fuzz of hair visible on his chin, although there was a look in his eyes that belied his youth. Trant guessed that this was the man Mrs Littleton had seen on the raid, shooting up the wagons. Apart from the colour of his hair, he bore no resemblance to Sim Morrow. As he dragged his horse to a stop the youngster drew a six-gun and levelled it at Trant.

'Why don't you take it easy, Jig, there's no hurry.' The speaker was a much older man, his hair and beard dark grey. Having issued this advice he turned his attention to Trant. 'You'd better have a good reason for being here.'

'I heard a friend of mine was around these parts,' Trant said easily, ignoring the antics of the youngster, who was amusing himself by levelling his gun alternately at Trant's head and chest. 'Just came by hoping to say howdy, that's all.'

'He got a name, this friend of yours?' grey beard asked.

'Several. I generally call him Davie. His second name's Gaunt, but most folks know him as Red.'

Jig snorted. 'Quit wastin' time, Fisher, I say we don't need no strangers ridin' in.' He kneed his horse closer to the grey and leered into Trant's face. 'Hammer ain't gonna like this feller, I can tell. He talks too damn smooth.' Swift and savage, he brought the barrel of the revolver whipping at Trant's face, but Trant was ready for him, blocking the blow right handed, his left moving across to snatch the gun from the younger man's weakened grasp and toss it aside.

Enraged, Jig launched himself out of the saddle. One solid punch from Trant's left sent him tumbling to the ground.

'I didn't come here looking for a fight,' Trant said. He addressed the words to Fisher, edging his horse away from the infuriated youth, who was scrambling to his feet, wiping blood from a split lip.

'Then what did you come here for?' Jig spat. He too looked at Fisher. 'I say he's here to spy on us. Could be he's a stinkin' lawman. Reckon we oughta search him an' see if he's carryin' a star.'

Quick as lightning, Trant swooped down on Jig and grabbed the bandanna knotted round his neck, pulling it tight. 'I've been keeping my temper, kid, putting your bad manners down to you being too young to know any better, but there's some insults I don't take. I'm not a lawman and I'm not carrying a star. You want to apologize?' He lifted Jig so his feet were almost off the ground, glaring into the youngster's face as it began to redden.

'Don't reckon he can apologize when he can't breathe.' Fisher sounded amused. 'Ease off, mister, an' give him a chance to say his piece.'

Trant eased his grip and let the youngster drop to the ground. 'Well? Have you got something to say?'

'OK,' Jig wheezed. 'I got you wrong. Sorry. Guess you ain't the law.'

'You guessed right. Forget it. I don't bear grudges.' He turned back to Fisher. 'Maybe I should have introduced myself. My name's Adam Trant. Any chance you people might spare a man a cup of coffee?'

'We'll take you to Hammer, it's up to him what you get.' The man wheeled his horse. 'I'm Zeb Fisher, and this here's Durdon.' He jerked his head at the third man, who still hadn't said a word. 'Reckon we can say you an' Jig already got acquainted. Come on, if we move fast we'll make it before the light goes.'

Keeping a watchful eye on Jig, Trant rode deeper into the valley, flanked by the three men. They reached a place where the trail appeared to end in a wall of loose rock. The side of the hill had been dynamited to form a barrier; there could be no direct attack here. The track that bent sharply around the rock fall wasn't wide enough to allow a wagon through, and a few yards on it wound around in the opposite direction. Here the way grew wider again, and ahead of them a rough wall had been built at the base of the cliff. A man leant over it and waved the riders on.

With the wall well manned, that narrow space would become a killing ground. It looked as if Hammer had made himself a fortress. Major Whitethorn had a couple of artillery pieces, and he'd been convinced they would be enough to win the battle, but unless he could find some way to get them through that narrow trap, cannon would be useless here.

'Just like home. Cosy place you've got,' Trant commented, as they rode into open ground, where half a dozen fires had been lit. He sniffed appreciatively; something tasty was cooking.

'We're a real friendly bunch,' Fisher replied. 'Climb down. Here's the boss, comin' to make you welcome.'

A man stepped away from the others grouped round a fire. A square built man this, not overly tall, but with a large round skull. He went bareheaded, and his hair was cropped very short. Unlike most of his men Hammer wore no beard. Fisher dismounted and went to him, keeping his voice low and glancing back at Trant as he spoke.

Hammer listened then waved his hand in dismissal. Fisher rejoined Durdon and Jig, and they and the four horses seemed to melt into the surrounding darkness.

The two men assessed each other as the distance between them shortened.

Trant judged that Hammer was a well earned nickname; the marauder's leader looked as if he would strike hard and fast, with no feeling for those receiving the blow.

'I don't know you,' Hammer said, having stared at Trant for a long moment. 'I don't like uninvited guests.'

'I'm sorry, I'd have sent a message on ahead if I'd known how,' Trant said. 'I'm looking for an old friend, and I heard he'd joined you. He can vouch for me.'

'Anybody gonna claim to be this man's pal?' Hammer queried, his large head swivelling as he looked at the men gathered around him.

There was a tense silence, and Trant's right hand twitched as the pause stretched a little too far for comfort. It would be suicide to go for his gun if things didn't go his way, but he'd heard too much about Hammer; better to die quickly than suffer a lingering death at the hands of men like Jig. A sudden laugh broke the tension.

'Hey, Adam, I reckon I had you worried there, huh?' Red Gaunt's huge frame came thrusting through the crowd, and a pair of strong arms was flung around him. 'Watch yourself,' a voice whispered in his ear, as the big man embraced him, lifting him clear of the ground, 'this ain't no Sunday school picnic. Hammer's a hard man to fool.' He spun him around to face the watchers. 'This here's Adam Trant. When things were getting kinda hot last year I headed north, an' that's where we met. Him an' me rode together in Canada, spent a real profitable year up there. If he wants to join you I'd say you were gettin' a good deal, Hammer.'

Hammer's eyes were cold. 'I got no reason to trust him.'

'I asked for Davie because a man needs an introduction,' Trant replied. 'It's been a while since I had a decent meal. I heard this outfit was doing well for itself, and I've always believed it's a good sign when a man earns a reputation. Be glad to join you, if you're willing.' He looked enquiringly at Hammer, knowing the next few seconds would decide his fate.

Hammer gave a brief nod. 'Maybe I could use you. But until we get better acquainted you can hand over that iron you're wearing.'

Trant smiled. 'Sure, but this gun's an old friend. I'll only let it go if you promise it will be in safe hands.'

At that Hammer laughed. 'You got no problem being unarmed?'

Trant looked slowly around at the gathered men until his eyes settled on Jig. He nodded at the youngster with a half smile, beginning to unbuckle his gunbelt. 'Ask the kid. I don't need a gun to take care of myself.'

Jig glowered, muttering under his breath, and Fisher guffawed. 'Ain't that the truth.'

Hammer's hand clapped Trant on the shoulder, 'All right, Trant, keep your gun,' he said. 'But you don't use it without my say so. Red, see that your friend gets a meal.'

* * *

They sat alone by the dying fire. Most of the men had gone to their bedrolls and Hammer had retired into the cave. As the man went inside Trant had seen the movement of something pale in the shadows; it might have been a girl, he couldn't be sure.

'If this is about that five hundred bucks,' Gaunt muttered, glancing around to make sure nobody else could hear him, 'then you're wasting your time, it's long gone. That's how I ended up here. I got into a poker game . . . '

'You were supposed to stay out of trouble until you got to Oregon,' Trant said. 'That was the deal.'

'Yeah, I know. I'm sorry. I can't pay you back, not now anyways. Best I can do is help you get out of this place with your skin whole, an' that's not gonna be easy. We — '

'Shut up and listen, Davie, I didn't come looking for my money. What happened to Sim Morrow?'

Gaunt didn't answer for a while. He reached for the coffee pot and poured himself a refill. 'I know you had your reasons for what you done to that kid,' he said uneasily, 'but can't you let him be? He's gone to Oregon, just the way you wanted.'

'You were supposed to take him the whole way,' Trant said harshly.

'Keep your voice down,' Gaunt warned. 'Hammer don't trust nobody, an' he don't sleep much. We want him thinkin' we're chewin' the fat over our days in Canada. Look, Sim was a broken man, he didn't care about nothin'. I don't reckon he'd have put up a fight if I'd drowned him at the first river crossin'. Last I saw, he was still heading west; he ain't gonna trouble you no more.'

'Did he join a wagon train?' Trant persisted.

Gaunt sighed. 'You always was stubborn. He got took on by a man called Toop, to help drive four hundred head of cattle to Oregon. Sim swore he wasn't gonna turn himself around, an' I reckon he'll keep his word. He'll be in Oregon by now. Leave him be, Adam.'

Trant stared unseeingly at the fire. Not only had he failed to find Sim Morrow, but by the morning he was likely to find himself in the middle of a war. It seemed that every decision he made took him further from getting this business finished.

'Leave him be,' Gaunt repeated, 'he ain't gonna bother you no more.'

'You were talking about getting me out of here,' Trant said. 'You'd better come too. Hammer's made himself a lot of enemies, there's an army on its way.'

'That figures.' Gaunt laughed. 'Well, I bin lookin' for a way to quit these bastards, reckon now's the time.' As he spoke there was a faint sound, high pitched, desolate. It came from the cave, and Trant swivelled to look that way until Gaunt grabbed his arm.

'Don't,' he said. 'Just keep talkin', Adam. Old times, remember?'

'But that was a woman! She — '

'Hammer brought her back from the last raid, over at Fullerton's cut-off.' Gaunt shook his head. 'I swear I didn't know what this outfit was like, I thought we was just gonna help ourselves to a few horses.'

So Shad Blazy was right, one of Wilkie's daughters had survived after all. 'Just one girl?' Trant asked, a forced grin on his face as he helped himself to coffee, aware that Hammer could be watching them from the darkness.

Gaunt cast a sharp glance at Trant. 'You know about that? There was two, but . . . '

' . . . the other one's dead,' Trant finished for him.

'Yeah, the younger one. It was Jig an' a couple of the others. Made me sick to the stomach. Wasn't nothin' I could do, though, if I'd stuck my nose in they'd have killed me too. I'd have left then, if I could, but there was no place to go.'

'I'm not leaving her here,' Trant said, his tone bleak. 'That girl's father went mad, Davie, knowing what his daughters would be facing. We have to take her with us.'

'You're the one who's mad! Hammer will skin us alive if we try a crazy stunt like that.'

'Not if he's dead,' Trant said.

8

Trant lay in the darkness, his body tucked up against the rock face. He had crept close to the cave entrance, and listened to the girl's muted sobbing as it faded into silence. A few stars showed in the sky, but little light found its way down into the raiders' camp; he guessed it was three hours before dawn. He was scarcely breathing as he strained to hear the faintest sound from the horse lines; Davie Gaunt had been gone several minutes, and so far there had been no alarm.

Despite the cold, the bone handle of the knife Gaunt had lent him was sticky with sweat in his hand; he had never killed a man in cold blood. Even now he wasn't sure he could do it, no matter how many innocent lives Hammer had taken. The fingers of his left hand flexed on the rough surface of the rock he had picked up from beside the fire.

Trant began to ease the stiffness out of his chilled muscles; he needed to be ready to move fast once Gaunt returned. At last a huge form moved to the last of the fires that glowed dully as they burnt to ashes. Trant came to his knees, not much liking Davie's idea of a plan, but seeing no alternative.

A branch was lifted from the embers, scattering sparks. Gaunt waved it into life, took a few quick steps towards the cave and threw it inside. Trant followed the flare of light. Luck was on his side. Hammer lay wrapped in his bedroll, his breathing slow and rhythmic; only the top of his bullet head was visible. Trant hesitated for a second then pushed the knife into his belt. He took the rock between his two hands and slammed it down on the sleeping man's skull. Hammer made no sound, but from the other side of the cave Trant heard a whimper.

'Is that you, Miss Wilkie?' he asked, keeping his voice low. 'Time to leave.'

The girl didn't reply. The brief flare of light had gone, but Trant could hear her quick shallow breathing as he crept towards her across the stone floor. 'Shad Blazy was sure you were still alive.' He halted a few steps away; the girl would have learnt to put no trust in men.

'Shad?' She sounded like a child, her voice high and shrill.

'That's right. I'm a friend of his. You have to be quiet, they mustn't hear us.'

'I can't come,' the words ended on a sob. 'He takes my clothes away at night. I don't know where they are; I've looked sometimes when he's asleep, but I can't find them.'

Trant looked back into the pitch darkness where Hammer lay. He felt his way back across the cave and rolled Hammer over, feeling the flaccid warmth of him and hearing a rasping breath; he would have to finish the man if he came to. The bundle of cloth lay beneath Hammer's bedroll. Trant pulled it free, along with a coarse woollen blanket, and returned to the girl. 'I'll be outside. You've got one minute. Wrap the blanket round you once you're dressed.'

Davie Gaunt waited by the steep track that led away to the north, the reins of three horses in his hands. Silently Trant gave him the knife.

'Did you do it?' Gaunt asked hoarsely.

Trant didn't answer, lifting the girl into the saddle. 'Let's get going.'

'Figured you wouldn't,' Gaunt said, nodding to himself. 'Hammer would have been a whole lot safer dead.'

'You didn't kill him?' It was the girl, and she no longer sounded like a child. 'You should have given the knife to me, I would have done it.'

Gaunt grunted. 'Guess you'd have good reason. No more talkin', there's two guards up ahead.'

They'd been riding for some time when Gaunt gave a sudden hiss of warning.

'Lookout post,' he breathed, easing

carefully from the saddle. 'There's no way we can get by without being heard. You and me will go up on foot an' hope they ain't too wide awake, Adam. You stay here with the horses, missy. An' keep real quiet.'

The crackle of a fire and the smell of coffee suggested the two guards had made themselves comfortable. A faint light flickered on the walls of a shallow cave. As he crept nearer Trant could make out the figures of the two guards, hunched close to the flames for warmth. He glanced at Gaunt and saw a red glow reflecting off the blade of his knife.

Trant launched himself forward and the fire illuminated the man's face as his head came up; it was Jig. The youngster's hand flew down to the butt of his gun, but Trant was too quick for him, putting all his weight behind the haymaker that landed on the point of his chin. Jig went flying backwards. Trant pressed after him, meeting no resistance as he snatched the gun from

Jig's holster. Turning, he saw that Gaunt had downed the second man; Fisher was out cold, a lump already starting to swell on his forehead. Gaunt shrugged as he sheathed his knife. 'Gettin' soft,' he said, 'I used the hilt. You . . . look out!'

At Gaunt's warning Trant began to turn. Jig's blow took him in the side instead of the back. Trant's clubbed fists knocked him to his knees, but Jig wasn't finished; he came back fast, the blade of his knife wet with blood.

Something flashed between the two men. Jig faltered, a hand moving slowly towards the bone handle that was sticking out of his chest, then he fell at Trant's feet. Gaunt leant down to retrieve his knife. 'Never did care for that little bastard,' he said.

'Thanks.' Trant put a hand to his ribs, where the wound had started to throb.

'That need seein' to?' Gaunt asked.

'It'll keep.' Trant said briefly, leading the way out of the cave.

'We'll put another mile behind us, then I'd best take a look. We have to wait for daybreak anyways.'

'We can't risk stopping,' Trant protested.

'Got no choice. The track's too dangerous in the dark, ain't a horse in this world I'd trust to get along it at night, an' I sure as hell ain't travelling the rest of the way on foot.'

When the grey light of dawn crept across the mountaintops, Trant got his first glimpse of what lay ahead and understood the reason for Gaunt's caution. The trail sloped across the face of the cliff, following a narrow shelf that climbed above a sheer drop to the rocks below.

They rode on to the path, Gaunt leading, and Trant bringing up the rear. In places the track was barely wide enough for the horses' hoofs, the drop beneath them deepening with every stride. Trant glanced back, half expecting to see Hammer's men coming after them; according to Gaunt the lookouts would be relieved soon after full light.

'We got trouble.' Gaunt had stopped, and the other two horses came to a reluctant halt on the narrow ledge. 'Come take a look.' There was barely room to step down from the saddle without falling over the edge. Trant eased past the girl's horse, willing it not to move. A landslide lay across the trail, burying it two feet deep under a sloping heap of loose rock. 'Can't ride over that,' Gaunt said. 'What do we do?'

'Only one thing we can do, if you don't want to start walking.'

There was barely room for the two of them to work side by side, shifting the rocks with their bare hands, Gaunt's great strength telling when they dealt with the largest of the boulders; he couldn't push it over the edge, but managed to heave it a few inches so there was room for the horses to pass. Trant was beginning to feel lightheaded by the time they were done. He stood up against the rock wall as Gaunt led the big paint horse onto the still-treacherous surface of loose stone.

The animal quivered, seeming to stumble, as the sound of the shot reached them, and then it was rearing on its hind legs, twisting, trying to get away from the pain of the bloody wound the bullet had torn in its flank.

The girl's horse snorted in alarm, springing forward and pushing past the paint through a gap that was far too narrow. Already off balance and frantic with pain, the big horse put one front hoof down on thin air. Gaunt tried to get out of the way, but he was knocked down the unstable rockfall, as the horse slid slowly over the edge.

Something whistled past Trant's head as he flung himself flat on the landslip. Looking over the drop he found himself staring into Gaunt's eyes, only two feet below his own. The man looked to be clinging on by not much more than his fingernails.

Anchoring an arm around the huge boulder they'd been unable to move,

Trant reached down to his friend with the other. 'Grab hold,' he ordered.

'You can't pull me up,' Gaunt demurred. 'We'll both fall. Hell, Adam, I weigh twice what you do.'

'I'm fixed to the rock. I can't lift you, but you can use my arm to heave yourself up. Move!' he urged, as another spent bullet whined past them, 'before they get close enough to take a decent shot at us.'

Trant gritted his teeth against the pain as Gaunt took hold, fearful that his joints might dislocate under the burden. With a grunt and a curse, the big man climbed up and across his body. 'Dammit, I had that cayuse three years,' he said. 'Ain't many that can take my weight.'

'Quit talking and move,' Trant replied, struggling to his feet, 'or you'll never sit on another damn horse.'

Gaunt took the girl's mount by the bit, with Trant riding close behind. 'You'd better take the grey,' Trant said, 'Miss Wilkie and I can ride double.'

'I'll be just as quick on foot until we get off this damn goat track,' Gaunt replied. 'Hell, what was that?'

A thunderous boom echoed around the mountains, going on and on, as if a violent storm was rolling up the valley. Woven around the sound was the frantic crackle of gunfire.

'Major Whitethorn just launched his attack,' Trant hazarded, 'he must have brought up his artillery.'

'So this is Hammer's only way out.' Two more bullets spent themselves on the rocks below, and Gaunt started to run, dragging the horse along with him. 'Dammit, we need to find some cover before one of 'em gets lucky again.'

They pulled up where the curve of the mountainside sheltered them from view.

'A few more minutes and we'll be in open country,' Gaunt said, 'but we ain't gonna outrun 'em for long with two horses between the three of us.'

Trant slid off his horse, holding onto its saddle for support as the world spun. 'You two ride on. I'll do my best to hold them off. With luck you'll meet up with Captain Orslow.' He dragged his rifle from its sheath and fished in his saddlebag for some ammunition.

'Be more likely to hold 'em up with two of us,' Gaunt suggested.

'Your rifle went over the cliff with your horse, you're no use to me with a handgun. Get the girl out of here.'

Making no comment, Gaunt followed Trant back down the trail to peer round a rock. Hammer's unmistakable figure was leading the way across the landslip.

'You shoulda hit him harder,' Gaunt said. 'He's got a solid iron skull, that's how he got his name.'

'Maybe I'll do better with a bullet,' Trant observed. 'Go on, Davie, get moving.'

The sudden sound of hoofbeats behind them made both men turn. There was a rider coming recklessly fast down the path from the north. His horse flecked with sweat, Shad Blazy pulled up so hard his mount almost skidded off the trail and into the chasm. He leapt out of the saddle, staring open-mouthed at the girl.

'Blazy!' Trant shouted. 'Here!'

The youngster hesitated, then ran to them, half his attention still on Jane Wilkie.

Roughly, Trant grabbed the youngster's jacket. 'Where's Captain Orslow?'

'He's coming. Maybe fifteen minutes behind me,' the youngster replied, his face flushed as he tried to pull free so he could look at the girl. 'You found her, I told you . . . '

'Shut up, we're running out of time. We need the troops here, right now. Take my horse, yours looks about done. And take the girl. Ride like the devil, Hammer's right on our heels.'

'I'll be needing your rifle, kid,' Gaunt said.

Blazy looked from one man to the other, and then gave a hasty nod. 'Yes sir.' He ran to fetch his gun, tossing it to Gaunt before he leapt on to the grey.

With the girl behind him he went racing off up the trail, the spent pony trailing them.

Trant lay behind the rock, just his head and shoulder showing. He drew a bead on Hammer and cursed as his shot missed. Gaunt was having no better luck, though their fire was slowing down the marauders' advance. A sudden flurry of shots sent both men ducking back into cover.

When Trant poked his head out again his appearance was greeted by a deafening fusillade. He snapped off a quick shot, having noted that at least twenty men had dismounted and taken up positions along the path.

'We need to get to higher ground,' Gaunt said, firing off a shot. 'They'd be easy meat if only they'd give us time to take aim.'

'Keep dreaming,' Trant replied grimly, glancing at the rock face rising above their heads. 'Unless you can sprout wings we're stuck right here.'

'You notice somethin', Adam?' Gaunt

said suddenly. 'Reckon them big guns just stopped firin'.'

'The only way the army could have got on Hammer's tail is if he didn't stay to put up a defence.' Trant felt inexpressibly weary, and the outcome of the fight no longer seemed to matter much. He wanted to put his head down on his arms and sleep. Perhaps that was because the night was coming — the sky was darkening. Trant's head was filled with the throbbing thunder of artillery again; with a sudden roar the world turned black and vanished.

9

Trant was reborn into chaos; he heard voices, but what they said made no sense. One minute he was riding across a vast waterless desert, his throat parched and swollen, then the next he was wading through deep snow, frozen to the core. Davie Gaunt rode ahead of him on the big paint horse, unaware of the man struggling in his wake. Left alone, Trant lay face down in the snow, and found Bart Wilkie's mad eyes glaring up at him from the frozen ground. The madman twisted the knife between Trant's ribs until he cried out in pain. Meaningless sounds echoed from a great distance, and Trant slid into deep water, going down and down until he knew no more.

The world changed. He was a child again, standing in front of his father's desk awaiting punishment for some misdemeanour, but before sentence could be pronounced, his father vanished. The room was empty, and yet the voice in his head was as clear as if the speaker stood close at his side.

'God may forgive you, Adam, but I never shall. I wish you were dead.'

He spun around, the room darkening so he peered through almost impenetrable gloom. And then he saw her. She sat in a corner, her head bent over the tiny baby that lay in her lap, its cap of white gold hair the only bright thing in the shadows. 'Dead, Adam,' she said again.

'No,' he moaned, tossing restlessly. A hand was placed on his forehead; it gave no relief, his guilt turning the cool touch to fire. Was that how he was to die, with the merest brush of her fingers? Trant strained to lift his head to see her, but when he opened his eyes he was staring into a black void. 'Lorena,' he cried desperately, 'Lorena, please!'

* * *

‘So, he’s decided to rejoin us.’ A thin faced man peered short-sightedly down at Trant. ‘You see, I’m a better doctor than you think, Captain. Few men would have survived the loss of so much blood. You may give him some of that water, Mrs Young, and the broth in an hour or so.’

An old Indian squaw with a wart on her nose lifted Trant’s head and held a cup for him. He drank thirstily before sinking back, exhausted by the effort.

‘I’m glad to have the chance to talk to you before I leave, Mr Trant,’ Captain Orslow said. ‘It’s a shame you aren’t well enough to join us; most of the survivors of the Littleton party are coming to Oregon with the volunteers, but I have my orders. I can’t delay any longer.’

‘Where am I?’ Trant croaked.

‘Fort Boise. You won’t be alone, young Blazy and his brother are still here. I’m afraid Dr Jones hasn’t been able to perform any miracles on their father, he’s sinking fast.’

'His constitution was weak,' Jones protested, 'it's hardly my fault. If you don't mind, Captain, I shall go and finish packing.'

Orslow smiled at Trant once the other man had gone. 'Finishing off the last of his bottle of whiskey, more likely,' he said. 'I wanted to thank you for what you did. I'm afraid we didn't get Hammer, but we've smoked him out of his lair. We killed five of his men and captured a dozen more. With luck the white Indians won't be raiding wagon trains again. The major appreciated your diversion; without it he'd have found it more difficult to take that camp.'

Trant recalled Hammer's defences. He almost managed a smile. 'Glad to help,' he whispered.

'I have to go. Call on us at headquarters when you get to Oregon,' Orslow said. There were a hundred things Trant wanted to know, but he didn't have the strength to ask. He was asleep before the captain closed the door.

For the next few days Trant could do nothing but eat and sleep. Mrs Young cared for his bodily needs but never spoke a word to him. Once Trant began to recover it was hard to keep Ann Geary out of his mind; he lay wakeful in the dark, wondering where she was. She must have travelled on with Orslow; she'd left without saying goodbye.

'Mr Trant?' He woke one morning to see Shad Blazy standing beside him. The youngster's face was grave. 'Do you still mean to go on to Oregon?'

Trant pushed himself up; his strength was beginning to return. 'I do. Is the trail clear?'

'There's snow on the mountains but I reckon we can make it, if we leave real soon.'

'Is your father better?'

Blazy shook his head. 'He died two days ago. Jim and I have been fixing up the wagon. If you're well enough to travel there's room for you. We've got two mules and a couple of horses, so we won't need to put your grey in harness this time. There's just the three of us; Jane went with the volunteers, along with everybody else. Me and Jim couldn't leave Pa. I swore I'd catch up to her if I could.' He chewed on his lip. 'She says she won't marry me, Mr Trant. But I ain't giving up.'

'Good for you. What happened to Davie Gaunt?' It wasn't the question he wanted to ask, but Ann's name stuck in his throat. He'd made it plain that they had no future until his business with Sim Morrow was done, but he hadn't expected her to desert him.

'He never came back to Fort Boise with us. Soon as Captain Orslow arrived, he handed you over to me and Jane, and hightailed it west.' The kid pulled a face. 'He took my rifle, and my horse, but I guess you never would have rescued Jane without him.'

'I seem to recall you were ready to make a trade,' Trant replied. 'So, he ran.'

'He didn't think the major would understand about him changing sides.'

'I'd say he was right,' Trant said, amused. 'Thanking him for saving my life will have to wait. He'd have been a good man to have along on the trail, but I guess we'll manage.' He leant down over the edge of the bed, fighting dizziness, and rummaged in a boot, bringing out a bundle of crumpled bills. He peeled off a few notes. 'That should be enough to buy two more mules, and some extra fodder. We'll want to make good time.'

'Are you sure you're feeling well enough?' Blazy looked at him anxiously.

'First light tomorrow,' Trant promised.

* * *

Although it tired him, just two days out from Fort Boise Trant was riding the grey; no matter how many blankets he wrapped around him, he almost froze to death lying in the wagon. An icy wind blew over the mountains, and sometimes it came laden with small hard flakes of snow. Since the days were growing so short, whenever there was light enough they travelled on by night. The blanket of snow came lower down the mountains around them with each passing dawn.

Five days out of Fort Boise, Jim Blazy pointed out a figure trailing them, a rider keeping about half a mile back. The next day he was still there, matching their pace but making no attempt to catch up. 'You think he means trouble, Mr Trant?'

'One way to find out. Tell Shad to keep moving, I'll join you in a while.' Trant turned the grey aside, waiting out of sight among a jumble of boulders as the wagon rumbled on.

'Hello, Red,' he said, his six-gun in his hand as he rode out onto the trail.

'Hey, Adam, what's that for?' Gaunt looked larger than ever riding Shad Blazy's horse, his feet dangling low under its belly. 'And since when do you call me Red?'

'Since you took to shadowing us,'

Trant replied. 'Friends come up and say howdy.'

'Hell, I'm a friend. I just wanted to be sure you didn't have any of them soldiers along for the ride.'

'They left Fort Boise more than a week ahead of us.' Trant looked him over. 'You're travelling light.'

'Didn't have much choice. I went back to the canyon once the cavalry pulled out, but they didn't leave much.'

'We can spare a meal.'

Gaunt grinned. 'I was hoping you could spare more than one. How about if I join you? Don't reckon you're fit to go huntin' for fresh meat just yet, I can make myself useful.' He patted the butt of Blazy's rifle.

'Sure, if Shad agrees. He might want his horse and his rifle back.'

'He can have 'em, just as soon as I get me somethin' better.'

'I suppose I owe you something for saving my life,' Trant commented, 'except that I paid out five hundred dollars on account.'

'I took Sim most of the way,' Gaunt protested. 'You changed your mind about him yet? I reckon you ought to give the kid a break.'

'If you want to stay you don't talk about Morrow,' Trant said. 'Don't push me.'

The ground froze, which made the going easy except where a thousand wagon wheels had bitten deep into the mud, leaving iron hard gashes that were impossible to avoid. A wheel dropped into a frozen rut, snapping the axle in two; without Gaunt's help they would never have hauled the wagon out and fixed the damage.

Trant had lost count of the days by the time they sighted the Columbia River. There were plenty of people camped at the landings, many of them boatmen and traders looking for custom among the last of the season's emigrants.

Scattered around the cluster of huts and tents were dozens of abandoned wagons, left behind as people took to the river for the final part of their journey. Those who remained on the Oregon Trail were waiting for friends to catch up with them, or building rafts to take them down the Columbia because they were unable or unwilling to pay for a boat.

'Sure hope you've got some money left,' Gaunt said. 'Unless you fancy we build ourselves a raft?'

'It would take too long.' Trant left Gaunt where an enterprising drummer was dispensing moonshine from a native tent, and rode slowly along the bank, looking at the craft plying for custom.

'You lookin' for a good boat, mister?' a one-eyed boatman shouted from the deck of his scow. 'There's one right here, she's a real beauty. Hull's as sound as a bell, shipped a new mast just six months ago. Could be your last chance to get downriver before the winter. Only gotta fetch my hired help an' we're ready to go.'

'I might be hiring if the price is right,'

Trant said. 'Tell me something first. Do you carry cattle? I need to know if a man called Toop come through here some time back, maybe six or seven weeks ago. He had about four hundred head.'

'Didn't travel none of 'em on my boat. Don't recall hearin' of anyone else takin' 'em either. Big herds mostly gets drove over the Cascade mountains.'

'So it's possible to reach Oregon without going down the river?'

'Sure, if you ain't in a hurry. Trail's pretty rough, ain't no good for wagons. You bringin' a herd to Oregon?'

'No, there's just four of us, a wagon and mules and four horses. Is there anybody around who'd know whether that herd went through?'

The man shrugged. 'There's a feller called Mo, lives in a shack up where the road forks. He knows the droving trails better'n most. Hires out as a guide sometimes.'

* * *

Mo was a Chinook, more than willing to trade information at the right price; he had no interest in dollars, and it cost Trant his spurs to learn that Mo had led the men driving Toop's herd part of the way across the Cascade Mountains. He also found out that a young man with pale yellow hair had been among the cowboys.

'Why didn't you take them all the way?' Trant asked.

Mo didn't reply, his weathered face inscrutable.

'I figure those spurs are worth an answer,' Trant said. 'What happened?'

'They don't listen to me,' Mo replied. 'I don't stay. They find the trail themselves.'

'What was it they didn't want to hear?' Trant persisted. 'That's a fine pair of spurs you've got there; you owe me one more answer.'

'They were in a hurry. I tell them wait, a few days. Stay out of trouble that way. The boss man says they have to get to Oregon, no waiting. They go on, I come back. Maybe they get there, maybe they don't.'

'What difference would a few days make?'

But at this point Mo clammed up, and Trant could get no more out of him.

Trant returned to the makeshift settlement and dragged Gaunt away from his third glass of rotgut whiskey. 'I'm doing you a favour,' he told him. 'It's likely to be a rough trip down river; you don't need a bellyache to make it worse.'

They spent the rest of the day stripping down the wagon and loading it on the boat and then they snatched a few hours sleep. The mules and the horses were taken aboard at first light. A silent square faced man had appeared, and at a word from the boatman he cast off the ropes. They began to drift, helpless in the current until the patched sail was raised. Despite the boatman's claims, the scow leaked in a dozen places, and the horses were soon standing in several inches of water.

'Well, just look at that,' the boatman said, pretending surprise. 'Guess you fellers had better start bailin'.'

Torrential rain fell all day and into the night, to add to their woes. They beached the boat before it got dark, and then couldn't launch it again until nearly midday because the water was running too fast. The following day the sail split, and the boatman insisted they couldn't go on until it was repaired.

With the frequent delays and the misery of being constantly wet and cold, Trant almost wished he'd ridden over the mountains, following the trail taken by Toop's cattle.

'Y'know,' Gaunt mused, 'I didn't care much for crossin' the plains, gettin' baked an' dry, an' the mountains wasn't none too friendly, but I sure as hell wish I was headin' back east, or just about anyplace except down this godforsaken river.'

'You didn't have to come,' Trant pointed out.

'Somebody has to keep an eye on you. I — ' He broke off as a sharp crack sounded from under their feet. The mast began to tip, then went crashing over the side, the billowing sail catching Jim Blazy and sweeping him overboard.

Grabbing a trailing rope, jerking it to make sure it was secure, Trant ran down the tilting deck. As the boat began to turn, at the mercy of the current, he could see the boy thrashing frantically, trying to keep his head above water. It was obvious he couldn't swim. Tying the rope around his waist, Trant dived into the river.

10

Trant thought he was prepared for the shock, but plunging into the water was like being squeezed in an iron vice. He surfaced to drag in air, his lungs a ball of pain.

Circling, pushing hard with hands and feet to get his head higher, Trant located Jim Blazy; he was only a few feet away. The boy was still afloat, thrashing with his arms, but his mouth was wide open in a silent scream, and he was losing the battle. By the time Trant reached the spot where he'd seen the boy, Jim had vanished below the surface. Groping beneath him, Trant located a handful of the youngster's hair, and yanked hard to get him back to the surface. He pulled Jim's head up and back, hearing the boy's desperate gasp as he dragged air into his lungs.

Jim Blazy was still conscious. With

the desperation of pure panic, he managed to turn himself around, one hand grabbing hold of Trant's arm. They went down together, the icy water closing over their heads. Kicking hard with his legs and trying to unlatch the boy's hand, Trant fought to take them both back to the surface. He felt the rope tighten around his chest; they were being towed along, and the motion was forcing them underwater.

Jim Blazy's fingers released their grip. Trant wrapped his arm around the boy's chest and held on, but he was losing his fight with the ice cold water; his strength was at an end. He gulped in a frantic mouthful of air. Jim was still in the circle of his arm, but he could do nothing to help the boy; they were caught in the fast current which was sweeping the helpless boat downriver. Tumbled over and over, unable to reach the surface, Trant could only hold on to the youngster and wait for the end.

As spots flared in front of his eyes, and he feared his lungs would burst for want of air, a large hand fastened around Trant's wrist and dragged him on to the boat. He hadn't noticed that the boy was no longer in his grasp, but the youngster already lay on the deck, unmoving. Shad Blazy came to turn the boy over, pummelling at his brother's back as he tried to drain the water from his lungs.

'Get up an' help me or the whole dang boat'll go,' Gaunt yelled, pulling Trant to his feet and giving him a shove. 'We're still takin' on water.'

The boat was listing dangerously, the top of the mast and a tangle of ropes and canvas dragging it down on one side so water was slopping aboard. Wild-eyed, the horses and mules plunged in an attempt to free themselves, hoofs slipping on the wet tilting deck.

Gaunt ran to help the hand who was trying to cut the wreckage away with an axe. The one-eyed boatman was screaming at him to stop, putting all his own strength into an attempt to pull the sail back aboard, but the sodden canvas was threatening to capsize the boat. Staggering a little as the boat deck pitched and rolled, Trant ran across to shove the boatman aside, sending him to the deck. Taking out his knife Trant slashed through the ropes, and the rotting canvas slipped overboard. Gaunt had relieved the other man of the axe, and with a single great blow he freed the mast. It toppled over the side barely making a splash, and drifted away. The boat righted itself, wallowing sluggishly.

Trant splashed across the deck to where Shad Blazy leant over his brother. The boy was breathing, but he showed no other sign of life, his face deathly white. 'We need to get him warm an' dry,' Gaunt said. He turned to the boatman. 'We'll have to beach the boat.'

'We can't land here,' the man protested. 'There's rocks all along the north shore. Hell, you can see all that white water. We're too damn close for comfort as it is. Anyways, I ain't wastin' no more time. Thanks to you I already gotta fit a new mast.'

As if by magic a gun appeared in Gaunt's big fist, the barrel held rock steady an inch from the boatman's head. 'If we can't land on this shore then find some way to take us across to the other side. We're goin' to tend to the boy. You don't want to help, that's fine, I reckon we can do the rest of the trip without you.' He thumbed back the hammer.

'All right, I'll land, if that's what you want. But you're gonna have to pay for that sail.'

'Get us down to the Cascades and maybe we'll talk about it,' Trant put in. 'For now, you do as you're told.'

* * *

The incessant rain didn't let up; they could find no dry wood, and it took a while to get a fire lit. Once the flames began to have some warmth in them, Gaunt went to fetch more fuel, while

Trant and Shad stripped the boy's clothes and tried to rub some life into his cold white flesh. They did their best to dry some blankets, wrapping them around his shivering body, and poured hot coffee down his unconscious throat.

The youngster's eyes flickered open briefly, just as the last light faded from the sky; he stared unseeingly at his brother, but he never spoke. Shad Blazy threw more wood on the fire, and then began pacing up and down the narrow strip of beach.

'Why don't you get some rest,' Trant said, walking across to join him. 'I'll watch over Jim for a while.'

Shad shook his head. 'Thanks, but I don't figure I could sleep.' He stared out over the river. 'I thought there wasn't supposed to be any place to land over there.' On the far side a fire blazed brightly.

'Maybe it was just an excuse. Our friend didn't want to stop,' Trant replied, glancing at the boatman who lay well wrapped on the shore, close to

Gaunt. 'Reckon Davie's right to keep an eye on him; we might have woken up to find the boat was gone.'

Sometime during the night Jim Blazy quietly relinquished his hold on life. They buried him beneath a pile of stones the next morning, then poled the boat off the shore and drifted on downstream.

It took them another two days to reach the Cascade Falls, two days during which the rain was unrelenting and the cold deepened. By the time they had unloaded the boat their hands were numb and covered in open sores. None of them had been dry the whole week, and Shad Blazy had a touch of fever.

'I figure we should leave the wagon right here,' Davie Gaunt said, as he heaved the last wheel ashore. 'Hell, we're nearly out of food, we don't have nothin' we can't carry on a mule. The damn thing's nothin' but dead weight.'

'What do you say, Shad?' Trant asked. 'We'll be faster without it.'

'I don't know,' the youngster said, his teeth chattering a little. 'Pa built it, and it's all I've got left. Mr Littleton said it would never last the whole trip, but we're almost there, and it's still in good shape.'

'A whole lot better'n we are, kid,' Gaunt agreed, 'but right now we need to think about gettin' you someplace warm an' dry.'

Even without the wagon the portage wasn't easy. The so-called road was far rougher than any they'd met so far. One of the mules had sickened during the days on the boat, and the first morning on shore they found it dead. Another was so lame that Trant had no alternative but to shoot it. At least that meant they had fresh food; the meat was tough but they ate it without complaint.

Mud lay deep on the trail. There were times when it threatened to swallow the mules, coming right up to their bellies. The five mile journey felt four times that, but at last they saw the river-landing before them. Despite being so late in the year, there were still emigrants waiting for boats to take them on the final part of their journey.

Riding past tents and a few ramshackle wagons, Trant was shocked to see how many of the travellers were sick; others seemed weary to the point of having given up. A woman crawled out from beneath a rough shelter and begged for food; Trant fumbled in his saddlebag and threw her the last piece of cooked mule meat.

Further down river there was more activity; several rafts were being built, one nearly finished and others little more than heaps of logs. As they approached the landing a shout went up; a boat had been seen, coming upriver. At once the work on the rafts was abandoned and everyone went rushing down to the shore.

'Dr Jones!' Seeing a familiar face, Trant dismounted, flinging his rein to Shad Blazy and pushing his way into the crowd.

The man turned, a smile on his thin

face. ‘Mr Trant. So, I was right, you made a full recovery.’

‘Yes, thanks to you. I’m surprised you’re still here,’ Trant said. ‘I thought you’d have been back home by now. What happened, did you get separated from the rest of the army?’

‘In a manner of speaking. There were boats waiting for us when we reached the river, and we were almost ready to leave when I heard that a man had been crushed while launching a raft; his wife came looking for help.’ He made a wry face. ‘Captain Orslow can’t resist a damsel in distress. There was no other doctor nearer than Oregon City, so he ordered me to stay behind. I only arrived here this morning.’

‘Do you know what happened to the Littleton party?’ Trant asked. ‘Did they go with Captain Orslow?’

‘No, there wasn’t room. They set off downriver before me, but I’m told nobody has left here for over a week; it’s late to be travelling and some of the boats are already laid up for the winter.’

He craned to look at the approaching boat. 'Excuse me, I have to go and see if I can get a place on board.'

Trant returned to his companions and told them what he had learnt. Shad Blazy's face lit up. 'You mean Jane could still be here? Reckon I'll take a look.'

'All them folks ain't gonna fit on that one boat,' Gaunt commented, watching as the boy vanished among the press of people heading for the water's edge.

'No, and I'm not prepared to fight for the privilege, so there's no point going down there. It looks as if we'd better find a place to camp.' Trant lifted himself back into his saddle. Despite his recent resolve not to think about Ann Geary, he found himself scanning the heads of the people scurrying towards the boat. There were very few women amongst them, and none he recognized.

'Kinda late to be heading back east,' Gaunt commented idly, as two men came off the boat, each leading two horses.

Trant grunted agreement, his attention elsewhere. There was a commotion in the crowd. Two men were fighting, and a ring of spectators had drawn back to give them room. It looked as if the contestants were unevenly matched; one of them appeared to be half the weight of the other.

'Hey, that's the kid!' Gaunt said. 'Ain't he got more sense than to pick on a man that size?'

'It's Littleton,' Trant said. 'Come on, I think Shad might need some help.'

Littleton had the advantage of weight, but he was twenty years older than the boy, and out of condition. Shad Blazy was piling into him, and by the time Trant and Gaunt got close, the older man was bleeding from both nose and mouth. The youngster was reckless, and Littleton landed a heavy punch that made him reel, with Blazy only dodging a second blow by a quick retreat.

'Coward,' Blazy gasped, circling, looking for an opening. 'You let her die, you yellow-bellied old faker.'

Littleton kept a wary distance; he was breathing hard, sweat mingling with the blood trickling down his face. 'I told you, it was an accident. Don't be a fool, boy.'

'What's the matter, am I too much for you?' Blazy yelled. 'Three women and a baby don't take so much killing, do they?'

Trant drew in a sudden breath, then he lunged on to the patch of scuffed earth, putting himself between the two fighters. 'That's enough,' he shouted. 'Shad, hold off a minute.'

'He let 'em die,' Blazy screamed, his face wet with tears as he tried to push Trant aside. The crowd began to jeer, not wanting the entertainment to end. If Gaunt hadn't intervened Trant would have been dragged clear so the fight could go on. The big man stood, head and shoulders above the rest, one hand on Littleton's arm.

'Fight's over,' he said, eyeing the suddenly silent mob, 'unless any of you fancy takin' me on.'

11

There were murmurs of discontent as Red Gaunt confronted the mob, but nobody rose to the challenge, and after a moment the crowd began to break up and drift away. Most of them walked away in silence, but as the men dispersed Trant heard somebody say, 'Are you ready to head up the trail, Mr Toop?'

Trant turned around, and found himself looking at the two men who had got off the boat earlier. One of them, a stocky black-haired man, nodded his head. 'Sure, Matt,' he said. 'Let's get started.'

'Hold on to Littleton for me, Davie,' Trant said, 'I won't be long.' He caught up with Toop in a few strides. 'Excuse me, Mr Toop? Can you spare me a minute?'

'If you're looking for work I'm not

hiring.' the man said, walking on.

'No, it's not that. It's a man I'm looking for, not a job. I was told he was hired by somebody called Toop, to help bring a herd of cattle to Oregon. Would that be you?'

'No, that would be my brother, and he's a long time overdue,' Toop replied, coming to a halt. 'I'm trying to find out why he hasn't arrived. Where did this man join them?'

'At Fort Boise. That would be at least seven weeks ago, maybe more. I don't think they planned to come down the river; they were using the drover's trail across the mountains.'

Toop scowled. 'So that's it. I wrote and told Seth to hire boats, no matter what the cost. Damn the boy, I might have guessed. I've never known such a year for raids on cattle drives, and I hear the wagon trains have suffered too.'

'I was with an army detachment that smoked out a gang of white Indians near Fort Boise,' Trant said. 'Maybe they've moved west.'

'How many men are we talking about?' Toop asked.

'More than enough to take on a few cowboys,' Trant replied. 'I found out that your brother hired a Chinook guide, but they seem to have had a disagreement. I gather the Chinook wanted him to call a halt for a few days. When your brother refused, he quit. He wouldn't tell me why exactly but he hinted that going on might not have been safe.'

'Then it looks as if I'm searching in the wrong place. I'm much obliged to you for the information, Mr . . . '

'Trant, Adam Trant. What will you do now?'

'I shall have to try the drover's trail, but not before I've gathered a few more men.'

'If you're willing, I'd like to come along.'

Toop looked him over then nodded. 'Be glad to have you.'

'I just have a little personal matter to

deal with first, it shouldn't take long. Where will I find you?'

* * *

Trant went back to Gaunt, who still had a hand on Littleton's shoulder. Shad Blazy stood a little way off, staring into the distance.

'What was that about?' Gaunt asked.

'Nothing that won't wait till we've talked to Littleton,' Trant replied. They walked away from the river, Littleton protesting now and then as Gaunt pushed him along. Following a little creek, eventually they were out of sight of the men around the landing.

Trant turned to Blazy. 'What's this all about, Shad?'

'They're dead. That yellow bastard watched them drown,' the boy said bitterly, glaring at Littleton.

'I told you it wasn't my fault,' Littleton blustered. 'It was a terrible tragedy, losing those poor women that way, and the baby, but it was an accident.'

'You're talking about Mrs Carlotti, and Mrs Jewett and her child?' Trant asked, unwilling to believe it.

'Yes, along with the Wilkie girl. They were on a raft, being towed bchind our boat. The rope parted and it was swept into the rocks on the north side of the river.'

'You travelled on a boat and let them go downriver on a raft?' Trant's voice was dangerously quiet.

'They weren't alone,' Littleton protested, backing away from his anger. 'They had two native boys with them. If it had happened in quieter water I'm sure the Indians could have brought the raft to the south shore, but the current at that particular spot is treacherous. It was bad luck that the rope frayed as we were passing through rough water.' Littleton retreated another step as Trant advanced on him.

'Three women and a baby, they would hardly weigh as much as a man like you,' Trant said, poking Littleton's ample belly with his finger. 'How come they couldn't get on the boat?'

Littleton stared at him, saying nothing.

'Tell us, dammit,' Shad Blazy said, 'or maybe Red can loosen your tongue for you.'

The big man grinned wolfishly. 'Reckon it'd be a pleasure.'

'They had no money,' Littleton blurted out. 'Apart from the Carlotti woman, and she didn't have enough for all three of them.'

'Yet here you are,' Trant said tautly, 'with a fancy silver band on your hat, and a watch on a gold chain there in your pocket. You didn't see fit to help them out.'

'We had to pay for the orphaned children,' Littleton replied, self-righteously.

'That's a lie!' Shad Blazy cried. 'I was there when the folks at Fort Boise took up a collection for the orphans. There was enough money to get 'em to Oregon twice over.'

Littleton glared at the youngster. 'The women weren't my responsibility!

If it hadn't been for me they would have been left behind at the landing. How was I to know that the river was dangerous? The Indian boys wanted a ride, and the captain did a deal with them.'

'That's the second time you called them boys,' Trant said. 'How old were these Indians?'

'I don't . . . ' Littleton blustered, licking his lips nervously as Gaunt cracked his knuckles. 'It's hard to say, but they must have been at least fourteen,' the man replied quickly. 'They knew the river. The women should have been safe. We'd have helped if we could . . . '

Trant grabbed Littleton by the collar and jerked him off his feet. 'I bet you never even tried! You filthy coward; you let them drown.'

'Hey, Adam, take it easy,' Gaunt cautioned.

'Tell me the rest,' Trant said, taking no notice of Gaunt. Giving vent to his anger was better than thinking about

Ann, dead and rotting in the river. He shook Littleton hard. 'You yellow-bellied piece of trash! Did you watch them go under?'

'No, they were still afloat when we last saw them.' Littleton was sweating profusely, his face turning dark red as he struggled for breath. 'When the rope broke we were a long way ahead before anyone noticed the raft had gone. By then it was already being swept towards the rocks, we could barely see them for the spray. The captain said going after them would be pointless.'

'And you were too worried about your own worthless neck to argue,' Trant said.

'You didn't see the raft sink,' Shad Blazy put in suddenly. 'Is there any chance they made it to the bank?'

Giving them both a wary look, Littleton grasped at this straw and nodded vigorously, his jowls quivering. 'Yes, it's possible. The Indians know the river better than anyone, those youngsters must have grown up on the water.

They might have found a way through.'

Trant flung Littleton away from him so he landed full length in the shallows at the edge of the little creek. 'Drowning's not an easy way to go. Give me one good reason why I shouldn't hold your head under the water and let you see how it feels.'

'They might not be dead. Maybe the Indians got the raft ashore,' Littleton spluttered, floundering in the mud as he tried to get up. 'Perhaps young Blazy's right, and they're still alive.'

'Stranded in the wilderness for a week and more? They might have had a chance if you'd gone back for them.' Trant made to lunge after him, but Gaunt's powerful arms fastened around him and pulled him back.

'Steady, pal,' Gaunt cautioned, 'I ain't disputin' this no-good skunk wants a kickin', but there's too many folks saw what happened by the river. He ain't worth hangin' for.'

Trant drew in a long breath. 'All right, Davie, you can let me go.' He shrugged the big man off and stared down at Littleton. 'Where did this happen?'

'Near a wide bend. There were high rock walls to the north, with waterfalls coming down. The boats all keep to the south shore, away from the rocks and rough water.' Littleton had managed to get to his feet.

'Exactly where was this?' Blazy pushed past Trant. 'How soon after it happened did you get to the Cascades?'

'I don't know. Two days maybe.'

Blazy turned to Trant. 'They could be alive. Don't you remember the night Jim died? We saw smoke. Somebody along that stretch of the river had a fire alight.'

* * *

'What now?' Shad Blazy asked as they pulled up alongside the wagon they had abandoned so short a time before.

Trant scanned the shore. The terrain was impossible for horses; they must either try to follow the riverbank on foot, or take to the water again. 'You'd better stay here,' he said, 'me and Davie will see if there's a way through.'

'I want to go with you.' Shad protested.

'You can't. If by some miracle we find them, we're going to need the wagon in one piece. And somebody has to look after the animals,' Trant replied. 'Keep a tally. If we're not back in eight days, try and find a boat to take you upriver; see if you can find them that way.'

The two men forced their way through the trees that grew thickly along the riverbank, clambering over rocks and fallen trees half hidden by the undergrowth. Every step was a struggle. Within an hour they were brought to a halt; a cliff face rose sheer from the river, and the water ran deep and fast at its foot. After this false start they turned to the north; it wasn't much easier heading for higher ground, but eventually they found a narrow trail and they began to make better progess.

Darkness fell, and the two men camped where the night caught them, creeping into a hole under a fallen tree that gave them a little shelter from the driving rain. Next day they pressed on as soon as there was light enough, their boots sliding on fallen trees and wet rocks, or getting stuck in deep mud. It was hard to say how far they had travelled. A third day followed, no better than the others.

'Adam!' They'd been toiling for several hours when Gaunt took hold of Trant's elbow and pulled him to a halt. 'This ain't no use. We gotta go back an' try the river.'

'No,' Trant rounded on him. 'There may not be any more boats this year.'

'There's no proof that fire we saw was anythin' to do with these women. Could be they all drowned days ago.' Gaunt pointed out. 'You still ain't told me why you're so hell-bent on findin' 'em.'

'You saw Shad with that girl. He'd be

out here killing himself if we hadn't come. I'm going on. You quit anytime you want.' Trant turned, head down to face the driving rain.

'Who's talkin' about quittin'?' Gaunt said, following him. 'But if we don't find some way of headin' south an' locatin' the river by sundown, I think we should head back an' try to get ourselves a boat.'

'Make it noon tomorrow,' Trant replied, shouting to make himself heard above the howl of the wind. 'I told the boy to wait eight days.'

As the day drew to its end, Trant hardly knew which way they were heading; they were in more open country, moving a little faster, but the mud was up to their knees, and his sodden boots were agony on his raw, swollen feet. At times he drifted back into the feverish nightmares he'd suffered at Fort Boise. He fell headlong, and was barely aware of Gaunt's hands hauling him back upright.

'We're stoppin', Adam,' Gaunt yelled.

'If you don't ease up you ain't gonna last until the mornin'. I spotted a cave a few yards back, an' there was some dry leaves inside. I reckon we can light us a fire.'

With warmth seeping through his frozen limbs, and hot food in his belly, Trant slept soundly. When he woke the fever had left him. Outside the cave the wind had dropped and the rain had almost ceased.

'Midday,' Gaunt reminded him, kicking dirt over the dying fire and strapping his pack on to his back. Trant nodded, wincing as he took his first steps and the sores on his feet opened up again.

It seemed that their luck had changed. A narrow track appeared, leading south-east. They were in thick forest, but animals or humans had been this way before, presumably blazing a trail to the water.

'Listen.' Trant paused. He could hear a dull roar from somewhere ahead. 'I think that's the river.' He increased his speed; they were heading downhill now, slipping and sliding as the track turned to follow a rocky gully. They walked ankle deep in a fast flowing stream; it would be a raging torrent in the spring thaw.

The track came to an abrupt end where the water dropped over a cliff. Looking out above the trees at the river, they could see where it widened and turned around a bend; on this side, the north, it was all rocks and white water.

'This is close to where we want to be,' Trant said. 'If they're still alive they'll be somewhere down there.'

Gaunt stared over Trant's shoulder. Below them a strip of thick forest clung to the narrow shore. 'Whatever made that track didn't come this way.'

'I'm not wasting more time,' Trant said. 'It's got to be possible to get down there.'

'Are you crazy?' Gaunt said, peering down. 'That's a hundred foot drop.'

'A bit more,' Trant judged. 'If it went straight into the river I might have risked diving.' He threw off his pack and clambered across the slope to his left, studying the trees that grew close against the cliff.

'Hey, what are you doin'?' Gaunt yelled.

'It's not far,' Trant replied, measuring the distance to the nearest branch with his eye. 'Hell, a child can jump four feet.' With that he launched himself into space.

12

'I can't do it, Adam,' Gaunt said, looking across the gap to where Trant crouched on a branch, searching for his next foothold.

'No sense both of us going anyway,' Trant replied. He left his fears unspoken; if their hunch was right and there had been survivors from the raft, that didn't mean he would find anybody still alive. It was over a week since they'd seen the fire, and that was a long time to be stranded in a wilderness without food. The women might have escaped from the river but still be dead. He took a secure grip of the tree trunk with one hand, holding out the other. 'I'll go take a look around. Throw my pack over.'

Gaunt obeyed, then suddenly his head lifted. 'I smell smoke.' He scanned the sky above the trees. 'There, upstream. Can't be more than a mile away.'

Trant paused as he reached the ground. 'Stay close. I'll be back as soon as I can.'

'I'll head that way,' Gaunt called back. 'Could be there's someplace I can get down.'

The smell of woodsmoke grew stronger as Trant worked his way along the shore, climbing over vines and dead wood that blocked his way, at times crossing fast running water, until he reached the clearing among the trees where the fire was burning. The place looked deserted, but somebody had put fuel on the flames not long ago. Trant hesitated; what he'd heard from Toop suggested the Indians in these parts were feeling none too friendly. He advanced cautiously, one hand on the butt of his revolver.

A strange figure, dressed in a ragged blanket and with a huge fur hood on its head, suddenly came running towards him from beneath the cliff.

Trant's gun was in his hand, the memory of Bart Wilkie still fresh in his mind. His finger was tightening on the trigger before a shock of recognition ran through him. The awareness that he might have shot her seized his heart in a grip as tight and terrible as the freezing river. Trant dropped the gun, and Ann Geary flung herself into his arms.

'Adam!' She clung to him. The shape, the warmth of her, the scent of her body beneath the filthy clothes she wore, were all achingly familiar. At that moment he was ready to forget the reason for his long journey to Oregon; nothing mattered as long as he kept this woman safe in his arms.

'I found you,' he murmured. 'Littleton said you'd died. I was so afraid it was true.'

As abruptly as she'd come to him, she pulled free and turned away. Trant stood bewildered for a second then went after her, putting his hands on her shoulders. 'Ann?'

She spun round. There were tears on

her cheeks, but her face was set like stone, her eyes hard. 'What about Lorena?' she asked.

He flinched as if she'd struck him. 'Lorena,' he repeated. 'How do you know about Lorena?'

'I know you shouted her name, a dozen times, when you were sick with the fever,' she replied, her voice toneless. 'I know she's the reason you came to Oregon. Who is she? Did your sweetheart run off with this man you've chased halfway across the country?'

'No,' he said quietly. 'It's not like that. Lorena's my sister.'

'Your sister?' Her expression softened. 'And it's because of her that you have to find Morrow? What did he do? Why are you so set on finding him?'

She was back in his arms, clinging to him as if she would never let go. 'You came back for me, Adam. If you're going to leave me again, at least tell me why.'

He shook his head. 'I can't. I'm sorry.'

Tears ran silently down her face. Trant stared out over the river, his expression bleak.

'Well, I guess I mighta known,' Gaunt's voice cut across the silence. 'An' you almost had me believin' we was here because of the Blazy kid.'

Trant turned to see Gaunt grinning at him. 'Not that you care, seein' you're kinda busy, but I found two women an' a baby on my way here. Seems they was too good-mannered to come bustin' in on the two of you.'

'You found a way down.' Trant pulled free from Ann's arms. 'Can we get back up there?'

'Reckon we could,' Gaunt replied. 'Except there's one little thing you should know. We got about a dozen redskins headin' towards us. They'll be here in a shake of a mustang's tail.'

* * *

'What happened to the Indian boys who were on the raft with you?' Trant asked, as he kicked dirt over the fire to extinguish the flames.

'They left the night after we were stranded here. When we woke up that first morning, they'd gone. We thought they might fetch help.'

'This ain't no rescue party,' Gaunt said grimly. He stared out over the river. 'Sure could do with a boat to come along right now.'

'We've been working on the raft,' Mrs Jewett said. 'Only one log was split, and we took that off and lashed the rest back together. The trouble is, it's too heavy for us to push into the water.' She looked him up and down, and a slow smile lit her face. 'You might not have the same problem.'

'How do we get through the rocks?' Trant asked.

'We've had plenty of time to watch the river,' Ann said, coming out of the rough shelter they'd built against the cliff, a small bundle in her hands. 'I've worked out a way to get into calmer water.'

With one heave, Red Gaunt had the raft in the river. 'You all sit together in the middle,' Trant ordered, as he gave Emma Jewett his hand to help her on board.

'Emma sits there, because she has to keep hold of Dawn,' Ann corrected him. 'Jane and I are going to help.' She met Trant's look, her large eyes challenging. 'We have enough paddles. There's even a spare in case we lose one over the side.'

'Just so long as we don't lose either of you over the side,' Trant replied.

'That's what these rope loops are for. We can put our feet through them while we're kneeling down to paddle.'

'Time to go,' Gaunt said suddenly, throwing his pack on board and leaping on to the raft so it tipped alarming. 'They're comin'.'

'We have to work our way upstream for about a hundred yards, keeping close to the shore,' Ann said. The raft spun as the current took hold of it, and then with all four of them paddling, the ungainly craft began to move sluggishly against the flow.

Something slammed into the log beneath Trant's feet, the sound of the shot echoing across the river. They paddled furiously, but with Ann's insistence that they must hug the shore, the Indians were rapidly getting closer. The savages fired as they ran, barely hampered by the trees that lined the narrow strip of beach.

'One of 'em could get lucky,' Gaunt growled. 'Adam, how about you give 'em somethin' to think about?'

'If I stop paddling we'll slow down,' Trant objected.

'If you don't, they'll be pickin' us off one by one,' Gaunt roared, as a bullet whined past his bushy beard. 'You two ladies, take that side, and paddle like hell.'

Trant threw his paddle down, drew his revolver and knelt facing the shore; a dozen half-naked men, their faces and bodies painted, were running along by the river, no more than five yards away.

Some of them were armed with spears, but several carried guns.

The raft dipped and turned with every stroke of the paddles. Trant took careful aim, drew in a breath, held it, and squeezed the trigger. The Indian closest to him stumbled and fell. Trant's second shot missed, as the raft gave a sudden wild buck. Behind him he heard a muffled scream and he half turned, to see Jane Wilkie sprawling face down. Ann was looking fearfully at the girl, the paddle in her hands immobile.

'Keep it movin',' Gaunt yelled breathlessly, his huge figure bending and straightening, wielding the paddle faster and faster. Ann obeyed, perhaps reassured to see Emma Jewett crawling to the girl; she had bound the baby to her, beneath her cloak, and she was keeping her back turned resolutely towards the bank.

Another man faltered as Trant's third shot found a target, but the attack went on. A spear buried its tip in the log close by Trant's knee, another skimmed between him and Gaunt and splashed into the water. One of the Indians dropped back as if discouraged by Trant's success, but there were still two alongside, easily keeping pace with the raft.

Trant had been too busy to notice that four braves had outstripped them, but suddenly Gaunt missed a stroke; he looked round to see the big man bringing his paddle down on the head of a man who was trying to climb on board. 'Adam!' he shouted desperately, 'there's more of 'em comin'!'

Trant ran to the front of the raft, aiming at the nearest Indian. The hammer clicked down on an empty chamber; in an instant the brave was heaving himself on to the logs, a knife held between his teeth. Kicking out with all his strength, Trant caught the man in the face; if Gaunt hadn't thrust out an elbow to save him, Trant would have toppled overboard. The Indian dropped away and vanished into the swirling water without a sound.

Looking round, Trant realized the raft was being swept back the way they had come, at the mercy of the current. A bullet whistled past; the Indians on the shore had a clear shot, and no longer needed to run. Gaunt was swinging his paddle at another man who was preparing to climb on to the raft. Trant grabbed the pistol from his friend's holster, aimed and fired. A black rimmed hole appeared above the invader's eyes, and he disappeared.

With Gaunt paddling again, his big frame hunched, the raft began to move in the right direction once more. 'We have to turn,' Ann said, gasping as a slug hit the wood almost at her feet. 'Adam, we'll need your help. Quickly, we're almost at the gap in the rocks.'

Trant loosed off two more shots, pushed Gaunt's gun into his belt, and grabbed the paddle. He was relieved to see that Jane Wilkie was on her knees again, pulling furiously at the water. A few shots followed them, but they hardly noticed; the raft jarred and tipped as it hit a submerged rock. Foaming water tumbled all around them, splashing across the logs.

Trant drove the paddle down and back, again and again, until it felt as if his arms were on fire. Now and then Ann would shout an order, to pull this way or that, as rocks loomed ahead. The dizzying motion threatened to tip them all overboard; it was hard to see where they were going, there was nothing around them but white water and the wet black rocks.

'Left!' Ann cried. 'Upstream. Quickly.'

Trant leapt to the other side of the raft. He thrust and pulled, gasping for breath. In front of him Red Gaunt was a blur of motion, huge shoulders straining, sweat and spray dripping into his beard. Again they turned, across the current, with the raft spinning and lurching, rocks terrifyingly close on either side.

It was an almost physical shock when the wild motion stopped, a startling change from chaos to order. The raft was drifting peacefully on smooth dark water, the north shore barely more than a blur far behind them.

When Trant lifted his head, Ann Geary was kneeling beside Jane Wilkie, examining the bump on her head. 'It's nothing,' the girl said, 'I hit it when I fell, that's all.'

On the other side of the raft Red Gaunt lay full length, his head over the edge so he could scoop handfuls of water into his mouth. At last he rolled over with a groan. 'That has to be the hardest thing I've ever done.'

'We're not finished yet,' Ann said. 'It will be dark soon. I think we'd better try to find a place to camp on the other shore.'

'That's no problem,' Gaunt said. 'We'll go pay our respects to young Jim Blazy.'

'Jim?' Jane Wilkie asked. 'Why, where is he?'

'Buried on the beach, right over there. He got knocked into the water when the boat lost its mast. Adam pulled him out but the kid died.'

'So Shad's all alone,' the girl said softly.

'Only if you turn him down again,' Trant told her.

* * *

The night was bitterly cold. They huddled round the fire, shivering in their damp clothes. Only the baby was warm, her naked body wrapped close against her mother's skin. Trant met Ann Geary's eyes across the flames; when she flushed he knew she was remembering the time when they'd shared their warmth that way.

'How did you know where to look for us?' Jane Wilkie asked.

'We met Littleton,' Trant replied. 'He told us you were all dead.'

The girl gave a bitter little laugh. 'That's how he wanted me, sure enough,' she said. 'I'm a ruined woman. He didn't like me travelling in his wife's company, in case some of the dirt rubbed off.'

'We were all a burden to him,' Mrs Jewett agreed. 'I'm no better than you, with a fatherless baby, no money, and nowhere in the world to go.'

'Don't talk like that, either of you,' Ann said. 'What happened to you was as much Littleton's fault as anybody's, Jane. If he hadn't been such a fool as to take that cut-off we'd all have been safe in Oregon long ago. As for you, Emma, I've already told you we're staying together. Once I'm performing again I shall need help with my clothes.' She laughed, looking down at what she was wearing. 'A great deal of help.'

Even in rags she was beautiful, and Trant cursed inwardly; in a few days he must desert her. He turned away from her to look at the girl, 'Miss Wilkie,' he said, 'we wouldn't have come looking for the three of you, if it wasn't for Shad Blazy. It was Shad who saw your fire, the last time we sat here.'

The girl lowered her gaze, not meeting his eyes. 'Mr Littleton was right about one thing, Mr Trant. I'm not an innocent girl any more. Shad mustn't give up his chance of doing something special with his life. He doesn't want a wife who'll be the talk of the territory.'

'No more than a few dozen people know what happened to you,' Ann put in, 'and it was no fault of yours. Anyone with a mite of sense will know that it doesn't make you any less of a decent girl than you were before.'

'I couldn't have put it better myself,' Trant said. 'Besides, Shad has made up his mind. He knows what he wants and he's not a quitter.'

Red Gaunt nodded. 'That he ain't. He was about ready to take on the pair of us when we told him he had to stay at the Cascades.' He rose, yawning. 'You reckon we need to set a watch, Adam? Only I'm about fit to drop.'

'Go ahead, Davie, I'll wake you later.' Trant got up and walked along the riverbank, thinking about the man called Toop and wondering how far he'd travelled on the drover's trail. By now he might know whether Sim Morrow was alive or dead.

'What's the matter?' her voice was soft and sweet-sounding, like distant music.

'You already know,' he replied. 'Ann, please, don't ask any more of me. I have to finish what I've started. I swear I'll come back to you, unless . . . '

'Unless you're dead?' she whispered.

'I'll try to stay alive. Losing you would be too high a price to pay.'

'Don't forget I shall be paying too, Adam. If you don't come back I'll be paying for the rest of my life, and I shan't even know why.' She turned away and left him.

13

'I can hardly believe it,' Jane Wilkie said, staring at the smoke rising from a hundred chimneys as the boat sailed down the river on the final stretch of its journey. 'A real town.'

'Best of all, they'll have a preacher,' Shad said, grinning as he put an arm around her waist and pulled her possessively closer.

'What do you plan to do now?' Trant asked, as Davie Gaunt came to stand beside him at the boat's rail.

'Don't rightly know. First thing, I'm gonna find me a decent drink, an' a meal. You still figure to go looking for Sim?'

Trant nodded, his expression grim. Gaunt opened his mouth as if he intended to say something, and then shut it again with a shrug.

An hour later Trant stood on the

quay, fumbling with the grey's reins. Ann had combed the tangles out of her hair and was wearing a dress borrowed from a woman they'd met on the boat.

'You look beautiful,' he said.

'Just about decent enough to introduce myself to the manager of Barratt's theatre,' she replied. Unshed tears made her eyes very bright. 'Please, come back to me.'

'I couldn't have a better reason for staying alive,' Trant said, lifting into the saddle. He rode away without looking back.

Toop's ranch was easy to find, but Toop himself wasn't there. The elderly cowhand tipped back his hat to look up at Trant. 'If you was hopin' to join him you're kinda late.'

'I guessed I would be,' Trant nodded. 'But when I met him upriver, Mr Toop told me he could use an extra gun. I think I'll follow along.'

'Then you got some riding to do, mister. They left at sunup. The boss was waitin' for the army, but he's never been good at sittin' still, an' there's been so many damn rumours a man don't know what's goin' on; some say there's been a massacre, an' that there ain't nobody left to bring them steers in. Don't rightly know what Mr Toop thinks, but he took six men with him, an' enough ammunition to start a war.'

'I'm new to this country,' Trant said. 'Where does the drovers' trail come down out of the hills?'

The old man pointed. 'The boss didn't go that way though,' he said, swivelling through a quarter circle. 'There's a track into the mountains further north; gives a man a view that's the next best thing to sittin' on a cloud. That's where you'll find him.'

After a day of hard riding, Trant saw horsemen in the distance, but they vanished into the high country; he pushed on after them until there was no light left in the sky. Next day he picked up the tracks of seven horses, and by nightfall he had almost closed the gap; he camped for the night and rose early;

men out looking for outlaws were likely to be trigger-happy, and it would be safer to approach them in daylight.

'I'd given you up,' Toop said, when Trant rode into their midst the next morning.

'Sorry I'm late. My business took a little longer than I'd expected,' Trant replied.

Toop nodded as Trant's grey fell into step alongside his horse. 'I was delayed too, waiting for the army. I decided not to waste any more time.'

'You're a long way from the drovers' road.'

'Only way to make sure we didn't ride blindly into an Indian attack.' Toop pointed at the broad shoulder of a mountain ahead of them. 'From there we'll have a view over more than twenty miles of the trail. And if the army are on their way, could be we'll see them too.'

'They were getting ready to march,' Trant said. 'Maybe no more than a day behind me.'

Toop nodded, and they rode in

silence for a while. 'This man you're looking for, the one my brother hired,' he said suddenly, 'why do you want him?'

'That's my business, but I'm not the law, and I'm not a bounty hunter, if that helps any.'

'You may not find him alive,' Toop said grimly. 'No matter what delays they suffered, the herd should have reached Oregon long ago.'

The ground beneath the horses' hoofs grew steeper. At last Toop raised a hand, calling a halt. He dismounted, taking a telescope from his saddlebag. 'Matt and I will go on foot from here, the rest of you stay put, I don't want anybody showing themselves on the skyline.'

'Mind if I join you?' Trant asked. 'I'll keep my head down.'

Toop nodded. 'Sure. The rest of you can brew us some coffee, but if I see so much as a wisp of smoke I'll have the hides off the lot of you.'

Crawling behind the other two men,

Trant drew in a sharp breath as the view gradually revealed itself. It looked as if they could see halfway back to Iowa. Far below them, the drovers' road wound through the mountains. Looking west, towards Oregon City, he made out a dark, slow-moving snake, meandering eastwards, a solitary wagon showing pale halfway down the column. The army were on their way.

Toop focused the glass on the advancing riders. 'If I didn't know better, I'd say there was a woman driving that wagon,' he remarked, before he turned the telescope to the east and scanned the broken country that lay below them. 'There,' he said, pointing to a dip half hidden amongst a scattering of trees, much closer to them than the advancing soldiers. A herd of cattle was grazing, with several mounted men keeping watch. The nearest rider wore a blue coat and a broad brimmed black hat; there was a distinctive tooled rifle boot hanging from his cantle. He sat very still, astride a tall black horse.

'That looks like Seth,' Matt said excitedly.

'Seth's clothes and gear,' Toop replied. 'There's something wrong down there.'

'What do you mean?'

'I taught my brother to ride twenty years back. That's not him.'

'That's not the only thing that's wrong. Look at the men by the fire.' Trant pointed to where four men sat around a heap of embers.

'Well, I guess if they've stopped to let the cattle fatten up some before they move on,' Matt said, 'they ain't got nothin' else to do but sit over their coffee.'

'There's no coffee pot hanging over that fire,' Toop said flatly, shifting to focus his telescope on the group.

'And there's something odd about the way those men are sitting,' Trant put in, looking sombrely at the rancher. 'I heard once of Indians using dead men as a decoy.'

'They're alive.' Toop studied the

group for a moment, and then handed the spyglass to Trant. 'Take a look.'

As Trant watched, one of the men shifted sideways a little; the movement looked all wrong, but it took him a while to realize why. The cowboy was hardly moving, yet his shoulders and back looked tense with strain. Trant studied each of the men in turn; grimacing, he lowered the telescope and met Toop's eyes. 'Their legs are broken.'

Toop nodded. 'One way to make sure they stay put. Whoever that gang are, they must know the army are on the way.'

'An ambush?' Matt queried uneasily.

'With those men and the cattle as bait. The soldiers will see them as they come over that rise, and to get to them they have to drop down into that shallow draw.'

Trant studied the place Toop was indicating; the ground was uneven and scattered with boulders. 'A hundred braves could hide down there,' he agreed.

'I don't see any braves,' Matt said.

'I don't think you will,' Trant said soberly. He had turned the telescope on another of the mounted men. 'I've seen that man on the sorrel before. His name's Hammer, and he's the kind of bastard who'd find it amusing to leave those cowboys starving to death with their legs broken. He leads that gang of white Indians I told you about.'

'Redskins or white men, the rest of them won't be far away,' Toop put in. 'Even from up here we can't see into every crease and gulley. There's plenty of places they could have pitched camp.'

Trant was no longer listening. He'd turned the spyglass on the column of soldiers. Toop was right, there was a woman driving the wagon. It was Ann Geary. 'We need to stop the soldiers,' he said urgently.

'If we warn them off, those four men will be killed,' Toop protested. 'I'm pretty sure the one on the left is Seth. It's his own stupid fault he's stuck down there, but he's still my brother.'

Trant studied the men by the campfire. He didn't think Morrow was amongst them, but he couldn't be sure. Even if Morrow wasn't there, he couldn't leave those men in Hammer's hands. 'So what do we do?'

'I've got an idea,' Toop said. 'How many cattle do you see down there, Matt?'

'At least three hundred head.'

'More than enough for what I have in mind.'

* * *

Trant followed Toop down a steep slope, careful to place each foot with care, intent on making no sound. Behind him he heard Matt breathe a curse as a stone rolled beneath his boot. Somewhere before them, maybe a mile away, the cattle were grazing.

The three of them had ridden on a narrow trail that twisted its way across the mountains, looping far around the place where the white Indians had made camp. There was no reason for guards to be posted on this side of the herd, but they could take nothing for granted. As the light faded, when they were a couple of miles beyond the marauders' encampment, they left the horses and continued on foot.

'You know what to do,' Toop whispered. 'Best if we separate. Stay out of sight and don't get too close to the herd. It could be a long wait, make sure you're well hidden when the sun comes up. When you see the signal, you know what to do.'

Trant watched the other two men dissolve into the dark. He went no further than the nearest tree, where he swung himself up on to a low branch, and waited for the moon to rise. When it did, he tried to pummel some life back into his frozen limbs before letting himself down to the ground. While he waited, blind in the dark, he had stretched his other senses; his ears and nose told him it was safe to move, but he took no risks, creeping cautiously from rock to rock and tree to tree, keeping to the shadows.

Alert to the slightest sound or movement, Trant grimaced, thinking of Toop's warning not to get too close; Hammer had Indians among his followers, and he was clever enough to make the best use of them. There could be outriders almost anywhere; by the time Trant found out if one of them was a redskin, it would probably be too late to do anything about it. That had been the reason for advancing on the herd separately; if one or even two of them were discovered, there was still a chance the plan would succeed.

The moon vanished behind a cloud, and Trant was blind again. He was groping in the dark when the slow thud of hoofbeats sounded from somewhere ahead. Guessing he had come across one of the men keeping watch over the cattle, Trant dropped like a stone. Wriggling forward he made contact with a boulder, and curved himself against its cold flank. Here he lay still, hoping the rock would cast a large enough shadow to hide him when the moon reappeared. The horse was coming nearer. Slithering a few inches and bringing his gloved hands in front of his face, Trant peered between his fingers.

Slowly the cloud shifted; a shaft of moonlight shone down, lighting up the horse that stood no more than thirty feet away. The rider was dressed like a cowboy, muffled up in a coat, and with a battered hat pulled low over his face, but beneath the coat his legs were bare, and he wore moccasins.

This might be what Toop meant by too close, Trant decided, grinning to himself despite his precarious position. He had no idea how long he stayed there, hardly daring to breathe and lying with his head on his arms; it was said that savages could feel if they were being watched, even if the enemy was out of their sight. Trant had no wish to find out if the story was true.

A while later, he heard the faint creak of leather and the swish of long grass disturbed by shod hoofs; the rider was leaving. When all was quiet, Trant began to move again, making his way south towards the bogus campfire; once Toop's plan had been carried out, those four men would be helpless to defend themselves.

Crawling on his belly, hugging what shadows he could find, Trant made his way between rocks and trees, until some sixth sense made him pause. There was no sound; it was more the absence of noise that made him uneasy. There were no rustlings of small animals, nothing to suggest the presence of the scavengers that escorted a herd of cattle on the move.

Trant rose to his knees, looking desperately for a place to hide. Not far to his left, beneath the bare branches of a dead tree, he saw what looked like a heap of rocks. He rose to his feet and ran, for now he could hear many voices, and they were coming nearer.

The smell reached him before he gained his refuge; this was no pile of rocks. There were splodges of white reflecting the moonlight, and strange shapes protruded in places like the deformed branches of some grotesque tree. When Trant drew closer he could see that one of them was a leg, still wearing a high-heeled boot.

Trant jarred to a halt. A face with the jaw missing stared up at him from the heap of bodies. Beyond that, the bloody stump of an arm reached skywards in appeal, propped up on a forked stick; either this was some macabre Indian custom, or Hammer had been indulging his sick sense of humour. Trant had no time to see more — there were men coming, and he was out in the open. He flung himself face down across the piled corpses.

14

The stench of decomposition was thick in his nostrils; there was a metallic taste of blood in his mouth, and it was not his own. Clamping down on his revulsion, Trant forced his body to be still; to move would be to die.

Many men were passing; one of them hawked and spat. There was an argument, three men disputing the bets they had made on the turn of a card, their voices raised, until another broke in.

'Quit that. We got more important business.' It was unmistakably Hammer. 'I want this damn patrol wiped out, every man and boy. You remember your orders. Keep your heads down and your mouths shut until they're close; make your first few shots count and it'll be all over.'

'What about Red, boss? You really

figure he's ridin' with them soldier boys?'

'That's what I heard. You do what you like with the rest, but there's a bounty for Gaunt. The man who brings him in alive gets five hundred bucks, and the same for his friend Trant, if by any chance they're still riding together. No man takes a woman away from me. By the time I'm done with those two they'll wish they'd never been born.'

This was greeted with a cheer. Sweat broke out on Trant's face as one man detached himself from the passing crowd and approached the place where he lay.

'Reckon we'll build ourselves a real big heap of trophies this time, boss.' The words came from so close that Trant steeled himself, waiting to be discovered. He had journeyed across two thousand miles of plains and mountains to end here — failure tasted sour in his mouth. It was hard to keep his hand still; he would go for his gun and pray that he could thwart Hammer's plan for him and die fighting.

'We'll piss on the whole damn army!' A strong smell of ammonia suddenly masked the stench of decay; the hiss of running water sounded loud in Trant's ears, until it was drowned out by laughter.

'You said it! We'll show 'em. Them soldiers ain't gonna stand a chance.' With cheers and curses the mob moved on.

Gradually silence returned, and Trant took up breathing again. With each passing minute he became more certain that Sim Morrow lay dead beneath him. His mission was at an end and he had failed. Lorena would never forgive him; if by some miracle he survived the next few hours, he would have to learn to live with that.

Trant eased himself up, fighting nausea as his hands pressed down on unseen horrors. A bird screeched and he looked up to see the first faint light of dawn streaking the sky. He waited, keeping company with the dead; if he could do no more, at least he would look Sim Morrow in the face.

As soon as there was light enough, Trant began heaving bodies from the pile; he had been right. There was the head of pale hair, blotched with blood. A cold hard knot buried within him was unravelling; the hatred between the Trants and the Morrows had run long and deep, and all through the months of travelling it had festered. He had made a promise to Lorena, but it had done nothing to dent the deadly Trant pride. Only now, far too late, he recognized his prejudice for the empty sham it had always been.

Trant reached to lift the body; a dreadful wound marred one side of the young man's head, matting the hair with blackened blood. As he took hold of one limp hand, he drew in a sharp breath; it didn't have the dead meat clamminess of the other bodies. Bending closer, he saw a trickle of fresh blood running from the corner of

Morrow's mouth. Hardly daring to hope, he reached to put his hand by Sim Morrow's nose and felt the warmth of exhaled air.

The slash to Morrow's head looked enough to kill any man; it wasn't surprising his enemies had thought him dead. Trant's fingers explored gently around the mass of dried blood and swollen flesh and he let out a deep sigh akin to a prayer of gratitude; beneath the wound the skull felt whole.

Trant checked the other bodies; but the rest of the cowboys were far beyond help. His thoughts were in turmoil. The name of Morrow had branded this young man a rogue and a waster. When he'd set out to find him, swearing to return him safely to Iowa, he had still been unable to see him as anything but an enemy. Now, nothing mattered so much as preserving the life that Morrow clung to, but it was almost full daylight; any time now the signal would appear on the mountain. Trant had come here to help Toop, and if the rancher's plan failed, Ann Geary would be with the soldiers riding into an ambush, and straight into Hammer's hands.

Morrow had survived this long; he must hang on a few more hours; his best chance of making it alive to Oregon lay with the soldiers, but for that to happen the white Indians had to be defeated.

Trant worked his way towards the herd of cattle, keeping an eye on the nearest outrider; a squat figure in a bloodstained jacket, he wore a hat that didn't hide his long black hair. Anyone who rode up the drovers' trail would see a tranquil scene, a handful of cowboys watching over the grazing steers. Trant stared impatiently at the distant slope. How long before the soldiers rode into the narrow gulley?

Almost with the thought, brightness flared on the flank of the mountain; the man Toop had posted there had lit a fire. It was time. Running, stooped low, Trant sprinted towards the mounted

Indian. A volley of shots sounded from not far away; Toop and Matt were trying to stampede the herd. There was a shout of alarm, followed by more shots. A man screamed and the cattle began to move, milling uneasily.

Skidding to a halt when he was within twenty yards of the Indian, Trant sighted along the barrel of the revolver. The man turned and saw him; dragging his horse's head around, he charged. Trant squeezed the trigger.

The horse shied away as the redskin slumped sideways and fell from the saddle, but Trant flung out a hand to snatch up the trailing rein, bringing the animal up short. Leaping on to its back, he saw Toop, still on foot but firing madly into the air; the herd was on the move and beginning to run but there were two riders coming, converging on the rancher, and there was no sign of Matt.

Trant spurred towards Toop, intent on rescue, but the man waved his arm wildly. 'No,' he yelled. 'Look!' Trant followed the man's gaze; there were four riders galloping towards the head of the herd; the cattle weren't running full out yet, they could still be turned.

With a curse, Trant dug his heels into the horse's sides, letting rip with a yell and shooting wildly at the nearest steer. The outriders who had been bearing down on Toop swerved to deal with this new threat, but Trant didn't even see them. He fired a rapid volley of shots as the cowpony leapt to a gallop, dirt flying from its hoofs. Already unsettled, the cattle thundered away from him. 'Stampede!' Trant yelled exultantly, reaching to his gunbelt for more ammunition.

Two of the men who had been trying to head the herd were engulfed in the red and white tide, while the others rode for their lives. The beasts wouldn't stop now, not until they had run themselves to a standstill; the marauders lying in wait for the soldiers were right in their path.

A shout came from close by. Trant

glanced back and saw the two outriders heading straight for him; the nearest of them was Durdon.

Trant swung the cowpony around. There hadn't been time to finish reloading, but he took aim and pulled the trigger; there was no sound, no recoil. The chamber was empty. Durdon smiled broadly, closing in, aiming low to hit Trant's horse. Desperately Trant wrenched at the rein, and his mount skidded back on its haunches, the bullet zipping past its flank. They were side by side and Trant slashed the pistol's barrel at Durdon's face. The man screamed and, as he swayed in the saddle, Trant gave him a shove which swept him off the horse's back.

He hadn't forgotten the second man, but dealing with Durdon had taken too long. The rider had brought his horse to a halt, and had Trant in his sights. Knowing it was too late, Trant lifted his gun. Time slowed. He saw the man fire just before he pulled the trigger and felt the jolt run down his arm. Something slammed into him; it felt as if he had ridden into an invisible tree. Before him, the marauder's face vanished in a spray of blood; a good shot, all things considered, he thought vaguely.

The clear morning had turned misty. Clinging to the cowpony's mane, watching drips of blood soaking into its rough coat, Trant rode back to where he'd left Morrow. He slid to the ground. Things had changed. The man was stirring, moaning a little.

It cost Trant all his remaining strength to heave Morrow into the saddle; it was lucky that he stayed there, just conscious enough to keep his balance. Trant stood by the horse's side, clinging to the saddlebow as the world turned queasy somersaults. To attempt the climb up behind the youngster seemed too much. Intensely weary, he pulled the horse into motion.

* * *

Somebody was shaking him, slapping his face. Trant stirred, wincing as pain returned with full consciousness.

'What brought you here?' Sim Morrow was staring down at Trant, looking like a man risen from the dead; he was pale as a ghost and one side of his face was clotted with blood. 'Why? Haven't you done enough? A hundred miles from anyplace and I still can't get away from you.'

'I had to find you,' Trant replied. It was hard to form the words. 'Pride, stupid . . . my father hammered it into me . . . the name of Trant . . . you've got it right . . . ' He knew he was making no sense, and closed his eyes for a second, marshalling his strength. 'Lorena . . . '

Morrow's face darkened, and he took hold of Trant's arm. 'Haven't you got your fill? Don't you get it? Beating me up and running me out of town didn't mean a thing. When you told me my wife and baby had died I didn't want to go on living. Ain't that enough for you?'

'I didn't know you were married.' He was finding it hard to keep the other man's face in focus. 'I'd been away over a year. Folks in town . . . when they told me you were living on the ranch, that she . . . They laughed at me; the head of the mighty Trant family, coming home to hear that his sister was carrying Sim Morrow's bastard.' He drew in a careful breath and shuddered; Morrow's grip was like a vice and the whole of his left side was afire. 'I almost rode my horse to death getting home. Lorena, I saw her and knew it was all true. I came looking for you without even stopping to talk to her. That was the biggest mistake I ever made in my whole life. I'm sorry.'

'You think being sorry makes a difference?' Morrow demanded bitterly, shaking him. 'Lorena's dead.'

'I lied to you,' Trant whispered, as the younger man's features swam and distorted. 'She's alive. And so is your son.'

'You . . . they're alive?' Morrow's voice cracked. 'Lorena, and the boy?'

Trant struggled for breath to reply.

'They were both alive and well when I left.'

'You bastard!' Morrow exclaimed, releasing his hold and rocking back on his heels. 'Give me one good reason why I shouldn't kill you.'

'I can't,' Trant rasped. 'Except that maybe you're too late. I reckon this bullet has beaten you to it. No hard feelings,' he went on, grimacing, 'if you want to speed things along.' He could feel Morrow's hand at his holster, and heard the faint rub of metal on leather as the man drew the weapon. 'Tell Lorena I'm sorry,' he said. 'And take good care of her. The boy looks like you,' he added, inconsequently. 'He'll not be a Trant, thank God.'

'Damn you, Trant!' Morrow thumbed back the hammer. 'Any man but a stiff-necked stuck-up Trant would beg for his life.'

'He won't. He's too proud.' Neither man had heard the woman approaching, but suddenly Ann was there, stepping out from among the trees. She was dressed like a man, though her long dark hair had escaped from beneath the wide-brimmed hat she wore. 'But I will. Please, Mr Morrow, don't kill the man I love.'

'Ann, are you crazy?' Trant tried to lift himself. 'You shouldn't be here.'

'The fighting's over,' she replied calmly, coming to kneel at his side. 'Hammer's dead. Red and I brought Doctor Jones; the sooner we get both of you back to the wagon, the better.'

'You don't know what he did,' Morrow protested, meeting her look.

'I do. Red Gaunt told me what he knew, and the two of you have just filled in the rest. But there's something you don't know, Mr Morrow. Adam was ready to die to put things right for his sister. Lorena's happiness came before his own, and mine. Maybe he deserves to be punished for what he did, but if you kill him you'd better shoot me too, because for better or worse, I love Adam Trant, and I don't know how I can live without him.'

Before Morrow could reply a horse came galloping towards them, skidding to a halt in a spray of mud and sweat.

'Dammit woman, are you loco, givin' me the slip that way?' Gaunt leapt from the saddle, his face redder than his beard. 'You — ' he broke off, taking in the scene before him. 'Sim? Dammit, you didn't have to shoot him!' He swept the gun from Morrow's hand.

'He didn't,' Ann said, standing to rest a hand on the big man's arm. 'It's all right. Everything's all right. Whether they like it or not, these two are brothers, and from now on they're going to be friends; Lorena and I will see to that. Come on, Red, help me get them both to Doctor Jones.'

THE END

Other titles in the
Linford Western Library:

CALEB BLOOD

P. McCormac

Caleb Blood was a man who'd seen too much bloodletting. He tried to forget, but despite the whiskey, his demons — past and present — wouldn't let him alone. All the things he should cherish were being stripped from his life. There was no option but to take up arms again. Once the guns were unlimbered, the death toll mounted and he faced so many enemies it seemed he had no chance of survival. When, he wondered, would the killing end?

THE BONE PICKER

Derek Rutherford

Sam 'Buzzard' Jones stumbles across a dying cowboy, whose final words set him on a course that will change his life and have repercussions for an entire nation . . . In the cauldron that is Bleeding Kansas, he fights for truth, justice and freedom. With a small band of allies Buzzard battles an unknown organisation — never sure who's a friend and who is a foe — and never knowing where the next bullet is coming from.

ECHOES OF A DEAD MAN

Terry James

Gambler and gunman Matt Lomew arrives in Garner Creek to recuperate from a near-fatal shooting. But then his childhood friend Jessie Manners is kidnapped and Matt is forced into an uneasy alliance with the brother of a man he once killed. This can only spell trouble, but there is no other course to take. As Matt races to Jessie's rescue, he prepares for a showdown, but he's not the only one being haunted by the echoes of a dead man . . .

PACK RAT

Colin Bainbridge

When Wesley Roach scalps and kills old-timer Pack Rat Dan, Jack Carson vows revenge. He little realises that he faces Roach and his gang of gunslicks, the local marshal and, worst of all, the notorious Canyon Kate. Riding for a rival outfit and teamed with the oddball Tombstone, Carson is forced on the run. Meanwhile, his boss's daughter Laura disappears. Will Carson come face to face with his target? And how much lead must fly before he does?